POETS AND MURDER

In Judge Dee's day, the literary world of Ancient China was one where intense study and almost ritualized scholarship were the rule, with academics and students alike dedicated to the highest concepts of beauty and art. But inwardly less exalted passions could erupt—to the point of murder.

During a Mid-autumn Festival in Chin-hwa Judge Dee is the fellow-guest of a small group of distinguished literati. Alas, he has little time for the criticism of couplets or calligraphy. A student has been murdered; a beautiful poetess is accused of whipping her maidservant to death; and further mysteries seem to lie in the eerie shadows of the Shrine of the Black Fox.

BOOKS BY ROBERT VAN GULIK

POETS AND MURDER

A Chinese Detective Story

by

ROBERT VAN GULIK

*With eight illustrations
drawn by the author in Chinese style*

CHARLES SCRIBNER'S SONS · NEW YORK

3 5 7 9 11 13 15 17 19 K/P 20 18 16 14 12 10 8 6 4 2

Printed in the United States of America
Library of Congress Catalog Card Number 70-161753
ISBN 684-16180-X

ILLUSTRATIONS

DRAMATIS PERSONAE

It should be noted that in China the surname—here printed in capitals—precedes the personal name

DEE Jen-djieh	Magistrate of the district of Poo-yang. In this novel he is staying for a few days with his colleague in the neighbouring district of Chin-hwa
LO Kwan-choong	Magistrate of the district of Chin-hwa, and amateur poet
KAO Fang	Counsellor of the tribunal of Chin-hwa
SHAO Fan-wen	Doctor of Literature, ex-President of the Imperial Academy
CHANG Lan-po	the Court Poet
Yoo-lan	a famous poetess
Sexton Loo	a Zen monk
MENG Su-chai	a tea-merchant
SOONG I-wen	a salaried student
Small Phoenix	a dancing-girl
Saffron	guardian of the Shrine of the Black Fox

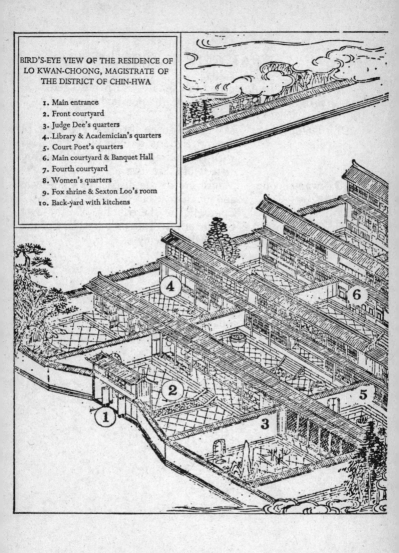

BIRD'S-EYE VIEW OF THE RESIDENCE OF
LO KWAN-CHOONG, MAGISTRATE OF
THE DISTRICT OF CHIN-HWA

1. Main entrance
2. Front courtyard
3. Judge Dee's quarters
4. Library & Academician's quarters
5. Court Poet's quarters
6. Main courtyard & Banquet Hall
7. Fourth courtyard
8. Women's quarters
9. Fox shrine & Sexton Loo's room
10. Back-yard with kitchens

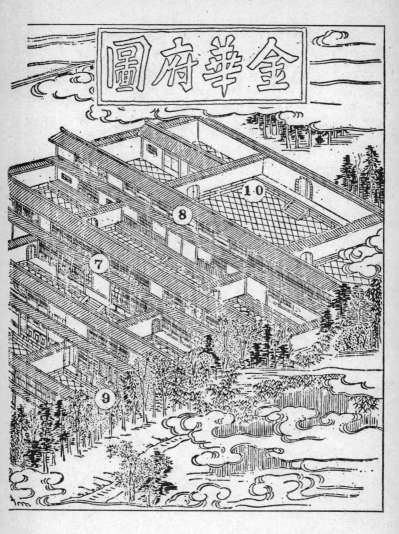

I

The obese monk, sitting cross-legged on a corner of the broad bench, silently regarded his visitor with unblinking eyes. After a while he replied in a hoarse, grating voice, 'The answer is no, I have to leave the city this afternoon.' The thick, hairy fingers of his left hand closed round the dog-eared volume on his knee.

The other, a tall man in a neat, black silk coat over a blue gown, was momentarily at a loss for words. He was tired, for he had been obliged to walk down the entire length of Temple Street. And his gruff host had not even deigned to offer him a chair. It might be just as well if this ugly, rude monk did not join the distinguished company. . . . He surveyed with disgust the monk's large, shaven head sunk between bulky shoulders, the swarthy face with the sagging, stubbly cheeks, the fleshy nose above the thick-lipped mouth. With his unusually big, bulging eyes, the man reminded him forcibly of a repulsive toad. The odour of stale sweat from his patched monk's robe mingled with the fragrance of Indian incense in the close air of the bare room. The visitor listened for a few moments to the drone of voices raised in prayer, over on the other side of the Temple of Subtle Insight, then he suppressed a sigh and resumed:

'Magistrate Lo will be distressed, sir. This evening there'll be a dinner in the residence, and for tomorrow night my master has planned a Mid-autumn banquet, on the Emerald Cliff.'

His host snorted. 'Magistrate Lo ought to know better! Dinner parties, forsooth! And why did he send you, his counsellor, instead of coming to see me himself, eh?'

'The Prefect is passing through here, sir. Early this morn-

1

ing he summoned my master to the government hostel in the West City, to take part in a conference of all the fourteen district magistrates of this Prefecture. Afterwards my master'll have to join the noon meal the Prefect is giving in the hostel.' He cleared his throat and continued apologetically, 'The feasts I mentioned, sir, are quite informal affairs, and very small. Poetic gatherings, as a matter of fact. And since you . . .'

'Who are the other guests?' his host interrupted curtly.

'Well, to begin with, there's the Academician Shao, sir. Then Chang Lan-po, the Court Poet. Both arrived in the residence this morning, and . . .'

'I've known them both for many years, and I know their work. So I can well do without meeting them. As to Lo's doggerel . . .' He cast his visitor a baleful look and asked abruptly, 'Who else?'

'There'll be Judge Dee, sir, the magistrate of our neighbour district, Poo-yang. He was also summoned by the Prefect, and arrived here yesterday.'

The ugly monk gave a start. 'Dee of Poo-yang? Why the devil should he . . . ?' he began. Then he asked testily, 'You don't mean to say that *he* would take part in a poetical gathering? Always heard he is of a rather pedestrian turn of mind. Dull company.'

The counsellor carefully smoothed his black moustache before he replied primly:

'Being my master's friend and colleague, sir, Magistrate Dee is considered as a member of the household, and attends all parties in the residence as a matter of course.'

'You're a cautious kind of chap, aren't you?' the other scoffed. He thought for a while, puffing out his cheeks, which made him resemble a toad even more than before. Then a lop-sided grin parted his sensual lips, revealing a row of brown, uneven teeth. 'Dee, eh?' He stared at his visitor with his bulging eyes, pensively rubbing his stubbly cheeks. The rasp-

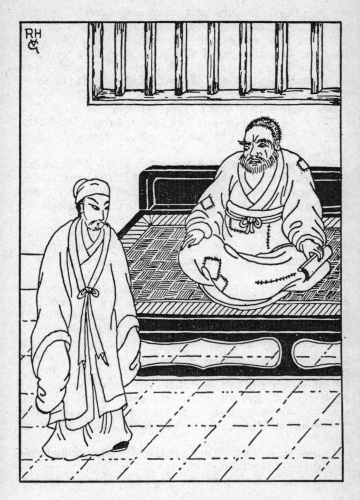

COUNSELLOR KAO VISITS THE SEXTON

ing sound grated on the neat counsellor's nerves. Lowering his eyes, the monk muttered, half to himself, 'It might be an interesting experiment, after all. Wonder what he thinks about foxes! Fellow is deuced clever, they say.' Suddenly he looked up again and croaked, 'What did you say again your name was, Counsellor? Pao or Hao or something?'

'My name is Kao, sir. Kao Fang. At your service.'

The monk peered intently past him. The counsellor looked over his shoulder, but no one had come in through the door behind him. Suddenly his host spoke up:

'All right, Mr Kao, I've changed my mind. You may tell your master that I accept his invitation.' Darting a suspicious glance at the other's impassive face, he asked sharply, 'How did Magistrate Lo know that I was staying in this temple, by the way?'

'There was a rumour that you had arrived in our city two days ago, sir. Magistrate Lo ordered me this morning to make inquiries here in Temple Street, and I was directed to this . . .'

'I see. Yes, my original plan had been to come here two days ago. But I arrived only this morning, as a matter of fact. Was detained on the way. But that's no concern of yours. I shall be in Magistrate Lo's residence in time for the noon meal, Counsellor. See to it that I get vegetarian food, and a quiet, small room. Small but clean, mind you. You're excused now, Mr Kao. I have a few things to attend to here. Even a retired sexton has certain duties, you know. Burying the dead, among other things. Of the past, and of the present!' A rumbling laugh made his heavy shoulders shake. It stopped as abruptly as it had began. 'Good day!' he rasped.

Counsellor Kao bowed, his hands folded respectfully in his long sleeves. Then he turned round and left.

The obese sexton opened the dog-eared volume in his lap.

4

It was an ancient book on soothsaying. Putting his thick forefinger on the heading of the chapter, he read aloud, 'The black fox is setting out from its hole. Take warning.' He closed the book and stared at the door with his toad-like, unblinking eyes.

'The smoked duck was excellent,' Magistrate Lo announced, folding his hands over his paunch. 'But there was too much vinegar on the pig's trotters. Too much to suit my taste, at least.'

Judge Dee leaned back in the soft upholstery of his colleague's comfortable palankeen that was carrying them from the government hostel back to the tribunal. Stroking his long black beard, the judge said:

'You may be right about the pig's trotters, Lo, but there were plenty of other delicacies, truly a sumptuous repast. And the Prefect seemed to me a capable man, with a quick grasp of current events. I found his summing-up of the results of our conference most instructive.'

Magistrate Lo suppressed a small belch, delicately covering his mouth with his podgy hand. Then he turned up the points of the tiny moustache that adorned his round face.

'Instructive, yes. Rather boring, though. Heavens, isn't it hot in here?' He pushed his winged magistrate's cap of black velvet back from his moist brow. Both he and Judge Dee wore their full ceremonial dress of green brocade, as required in the presence of the Prefect, their direct chief. It had been a crisp and cool autumn morning, but now the strong rays of the midday sun were beating on the palankeen's roof.

Lo yawned. 'Well, now that the conference is over and done with, Dee, we can turn our minds to more pleasant subjects! I have drawn up a detailed programme for the two days you'll be honouring me with your presence, elder brother! Rather a nice programme, though I say so myself!'

'I hate to impose on your hospitality, Lo! Please don't go to any trouble on my account. If I can read a bit in your fine library, I . . .'

'You won't have much time for reading, my dear fellow!' Lo drew the window curtain open. The palankeen was passing through the main street. Magistrate Lo pointed at the shop fronts, gaily decorated with coloured lampions of all shapes and sizes. 'Tomorrow is the Mid-autumn Festival! We'll start celebrating this very night! With a dinner party. Small but select!'

Judge Dee smiled politely, but his colleague's mentioning the Mid-autumn Festival had given him a sudden pang of regret. More than any of the many calendar feasts this one was a household affair, presided over by one's womenfolk, and in which the children also took a large part. The judge had been looking forward to celebrating this feast in Poo-yang in the intimacy of his own family circle. But the Prefect had ordered him to stay on for two days in Chin-hwa, so as to be on hand if the Prefect, who was going back to the provincial capital the next week, should want to summon him again. Judge Dee sighed. He would have much preferred to return to Poo-yang at once, not only because of the festival, but also because a complicated case of fraud was pending in his tribunal and he wanted to attend to it personally. Because of this case he had decided to travel to Chin-hwa alone, leaving his trusted adviser Sergeant Hoong and his three lieutenants in Poo-yang so that they could gather all the data for the final indictment. 'Eh, who did you say?'

'The Academician Shao, my dear fellow! He has consented to honour my poor dwelling with his presence!'

'You don't mean the former President of the Academy? The man who until recently drafted all the more important imperial edicts?'

Magistrate Lo smiled broadly.

'Yes indeed! One of the greatest writers of our time, both

in poetry and prose. Then the Court Poet, the honourable Chang Lan-po, will also be staying with us.'

'Heavens, another illustrious name! You really shouldn't call yourself an amateur, Lo! That these famous poets come to stay with you proves that you . . .'

His portly colleague quickly raised his hand.

'Oh no, Dee, no such luck! Mere accident! The Academician happened to be passing through here on his way back to the capital. And Chang, having been born and bred here in Chin-hwa, has come to worship at his ancestral shrine. Now, as you know, the tribunal here, including my official residence, is a former princely summer palace; it used to belong to the notorious Ninth Prince, who planned to usurp the throne, twenty years ago. There are many separate courtyards, and nice gardens too. The two distinguished gentlemen accepted my invitation only because they thought they'd be more comfortable with me than in a hostel!'

'You're much too modest, Lo! Both Shao and Chang are men of fastidious taste, they'd never have accepted your invitation to stay with you if they hadn't been impressed by your elegant poetry. When will they arrive?'

'They should be there right now, elder brother! Told my housemaster to serve them the noon meal in the main hall, my counsellor deputizing for me as host. I think we'll be there soon.' He drew the window curtain aside. 'Heavens, what is Kao doing there?' Poking his head out of the window, he shouted at the foreman of the palankeen bearers: 'Stop!'

While the palankeen was being lowered to the ground in front of the main gate of the tribunal, Judge Dee saw through the window an uneasy group of people standing close together on the broad steps. The neat man in the black coat and blue gown he recognized as Lo's counsellor, Kao. The lean fellow, wearing a black-bordered brown jacket and trousers and a black-lacquered helmet with a long red tassel, had to be the headman of the constables. The two others seemed ordinary citizens. Three constables stood somewhat apart. They wore the same uniform as their headman, but their helmets lacked the red tassel. They had thin chains round their waists, from which dangled thumbscrews and manacles. Kao came quickly down the stairs and made a low bow in front of the palankeen window. Magistrate Lo asked curtly:

'What's up, Kao?'

'Half an hour ago the steward of Mr Meng the tea-merchant came to report a murder, sir. Mr Soong, the student who is renting the back courtyard of Meng's residence, was found with his throat cut. All his money has been stolen. Seems to have happened very early this morning, sir.'

'A murder on the eve of the festival! Of all the bad luck!' Lo muttered to Judge Dee. Then he asked Kao with a worried look, 'What about my guests?'

'His Excellency the Academician Shao arrived just after you had left, sir, followed by the Honourable Chang. I showed the gentlemen their quarters, apologizing for Your Honour's absence. Just when they were sitting down to the noon meal, Sexton Loo made his appearance. After the meal the three gentlemen retired for their siesta.'

'Good. That means that I can go at once to inspect the scene of the crime. Plenty of time to welcome my guests after the siesta. Send the headman and a couple of constables ahead on horseback, Kao. Let them see to it that nobody messes things up, eh. Did you warn the coroner?'

'Yes, sir. I also took from our files the papers relating to the victim, and to his landlord, Merchant Meng.' He pulled a sheaf of official documents from his sleeve and handed them respectfully to his chief.

'Good work! You stay here in the tribunal, Kao. See whether any important papers have come in and deal with the routine matters!' He barked at the foreman of the bearers who had been listening avidly, 'You know Mr Meng's place? Near the East Gate, you say? All right, get a move on!'

9

As the palankeen was being carried away, Lo laid his hand on Judge Dee's arm and said quickly:

'Hope you don't mind missing your siesta, Dee! Need your help and advice, you know. Couldn't possibly deal with a murder all alone on a full stomach. Should've gone easy on the wine. Had just that one cup too many, I fear!' He wiped the perspiration from his face and asked again with an anxious look, 'You really don't mind, do you, Dee?'

'Of course not. I'll be glad to do what I can.' The judge stroked his moustache, then added dryly, 'Especially since I'll be on the spot with you, Lo. So that you can't pull the wool over my eyes, as you did on Paradise Island recently!'

'Well, you weren't too communicative either, elder brother! Last year, I mean. When you came to snatch those two nice girls away from here!'*

Judge Dee smiled bleakly.

'All right, let's say we're quits! I expect this'll be just a routine case, though. Most murders for robbery are. Let's see exactly who the victim was.'

Lo quickly pushed the sheaf of papers into his colleague's hands. 'You have a look first, elder brother! I'll just shut my eyes for a moment or two. To concentrate my thoughts, you see. It's quite a long way to the East Gate.' He pushed his cap well forward over his eyes and leaned back in the cushions with a contented sigh.

The judge drew open the window curtain on his side to get a better light to read by. Before starting, however, he bestowed a thoughtful look on the flushed face of his colleague. It would be interesting to see how Lo would go about a murder investigation. He reflected that a magistrate, not being allowed to leave his own district without express orders from the Prefect, had but rarely an opportunity to see a colleague at work. Besides, Lo was quite an unusual person. He possessed ample

---

* See the novels The Red Pavilion and The Chinese Bell Murders.

private means, and rumour had it that he had accepted the magistracy of Chin-hwa only because it gave him an independent official position, and opportunity for indulging in his hobbies of wine, women and poetry. Chin-hwa was always a difficult post to fill, because only a magistrate with a large private income could properly keep up the palatial residence, and it was whispered in official circles that it was chiefly for that reason that Lo was maintained in the post. But Judge Dee often suspected that Lo's air of being a *bon viveur*, without interest in official duties, was largely assumed and carefully cultivated, and that in fact he administered his district rather well. And just now he had been favourably impressed by his colleague's decision to proceed to the scene of the crime himself. Many a magistrate would have left the routine examination on the spot to his underlings. The judge unrolled the documents. On top was a paper giving the official particulars about the murdered student.

His full name was Soong I-wen; twenty-three years of age and unmarried. Having passed the second literary examination with honours, he had been granted a scholarship, so as to enable him to edit a section of an old dynastic history. Soong had come to Chin-hwa two weeks previously, and he had registered at once in the tribunal, applying for permission to stay one month. He had explained to Counsellor Kao that the purpose of his visit was to consult the local historical records. A few centuries before, exactly in the period Soong was studying, there had occurred a peasant revolt in Chin-hwa, and Soong hoped to find additional data on that event in the old archives. The counsellor had issued a permit allowing him to consult the files in the chancery. From the list of visits appended, it appeared that Soong had passed every afternoon in the tribunal's library. That was all.

The other papers related to the student's landlord, the tea-merchant Meng Su-chai. Meng had taken over the old-established tea firm from his father. Eighteen years ago he had

11

A MERCHANT WELCOMES TWO MAGISTRATES

married the daughter of a colleague called Hwang, who had borne him a daughter, now sixteen, and a son, fourteen. He had one officially registered concubine. Marriage and birth certificates were attached. Judge Dee nodded with satisfaction; Counsellor Kao was evidently a diligent officer. Merchant Meng was forty now; he paid his taxes on time and supported a few charitable organizations. He was evidently a Buddhist, for he was a patron of the Temple of Subtle Insight, one of the many sanctuaries in Temple Street. Thinking of Buddhism reminded the judge of something. He nudged his companion who was snoring softly and asked, 'What did your counsellor say about a sexton?'

'A sexton?' Lo stared at him with sleep-heavy eyes.

'Didn't I hear Kao mention that a sexton took part in to-day's noon meal in your residence?'

'Of course! You must have heard of Sexton Loo, haven't you?'

'No, I haven't. I don't mix much with the Buddhist crowd.' As a staunch Confucianist, Judge Dee disapproved of Buddhism, and the scandalous behaviour of the monks in the Temple of Transcendental Wisdom in his own district had further fortified him in this antagonistic attitude.

Magistrate Lo chuckled.

'Sexton Loo doesn't belong to any crowd, Dee. Will be a real treat for you to meet him, elder brother! You'll positively enjoy talking with him. My head feels a bit better now. Let me have a look at those documents!'

Judge Dee handed him the sheaf of papers, and sat back in silence for the remainder of the journey.

III

The tea-merchant's house was located in a lane so narrow
that the palankeen could hardly pass, but the high brick walls
on both sides, decked with weatherbeaten green tiles, indicated that this was an old residential section of the town, in-
habited by well-to-do people. The bearers halted in front of
a black-lacquered gate, lavishly decorated with metal work.
The headman who stood waiting there raised his whip, and
the small crowd of curious onlookers scattered. The double-
gate was pushed open. The high canopy of the palankeen just
cleared the heavy age-blackened rafters of the gatehouse.

Stepping down from the palankeen after Magistrate Lo,
Judge Dee threw a quick look at the well-kept front courtyard, quiet and cool in the shadow of two tall yew trees. They
flanked the granite steps leading up to the impressive, red-
pillared main hall. A thin man dressed in a long, olive-green
gown and wearing a square black cap of pleated horsehair
came hurriedly down the stairs to welcome the visitors. Lo
went up to him with quick, mincing steps.

'You are the merchant Meng, I presume? Splendid! Glad
to meet the owner of our most famous tea firm. Terrible thing,
murder and robbery in your old-established, distinguished
house! And on the eve of the Mid-autumn Festival, too!'

Mr Meng made a low bow and began to apologize for the
trouble he was causing the authorities. But the small magistrate cut him short.

'Always at the citizens' service, Mr Meng! Always! This
gentleman is a friend of mine, by the way. A colleague who
happened to be with me when the murder was reported.' Lo
put his winged cap at a jaunty angle. 'Well, take us to the
place where it happened. Your back-courtyard, if I remember
correctly.'

'Indeed, Your Honour. May I be allowed to offer some refreshments in the main hall first? Then I can explain to Your Honour exactly how . . .'

'No, no need to stand on ceremony, my dear fellow! Lead the way to the back-yard, please.'

The tea-merchant's face fell, but he made a resigned bow and took them along a covered corridor that went round the main hall to a walled garden at the back, lined by rows of potted flowers. Two maidservants scurried away when they saw their master and the two high officials coming round the corner. The headman brought up the rear, the iron manacles suspended on his belt clanking together at his every step. Mr Meng pointed at the sprawling building opposite.

'Those are my family quarters, sir. We'll go round them by the pathway on the left here.'

Walking along the narrow paved path which ran under the protruding eaves, close to the red-lacquered lattice windows, Judge Dee got a glimpse of a pale face inside. He thought it was a young and rather handsome girl.

They came to an extensive orchard where a variety of fruit trees stood in tangled undergrowth.

'My late mother was greatly interested in the cultivation of trees and plants,' the tea-merchant explained. 'She personally supervised the gardeners. After her demise last year, I couldn't find time . . .'

'Quite,' Magistrate Lo said, gathering up the lower hem of his robe. The winding footpath leading through the orchard was lined by thorny weeds. 'Those pears up there look delicious.'

'It's a special kind, Your Honour. Large and tasty. Well, the back-yard rented by Mr Soong is over on the other side there, you can just see the roof. Your Honour'll understand now why we didn't hear any outcry or commotion at midnight. We . . .'

Lo halted in his steps.

15

'Last night? Why then was the murder reported only this noon?'

'That was the time the body was discovered, sir. Mr Soong always breakfasted on a few oil-cakes from the stall on the corner, and he used to brew his own morning tea. But his noon and evening rice were served by my maids. When Soong didn't open up when the maid brought his noon meal, she fetched me. I knocked several times, and called Mr Soong's name. When no sound came from inside I feared he had fallen seriously ill. I ordered my steward to break the door down and . . .'

'I see. Well, let's go on!'

A constable was guarding the door of the low brick building at the back of the orchard. He opened the door carefully, for the panel was cracked and the hinges out of joint. As they stepped inside the small library, the tea-merchant said vexedly:

'Look how the murderer ransacked the place, sir! And it was my late mother's favourite room. After my father's death she came here nearly every afternoon—it was so quiet, and she could see her trees right in front of the window. She sat here at the desk, reading and writing. And now . . .' He cast a dejected glance at the rosewood desk by the window. The drawers had been pulled out, their contents strewn on the paved floor: papers, visiting-cards, and writing implements. Beside the cushioned armchair lay a red leather cash-box, the lid half wrenched off. It was empty.

'I see that madame your mother liked poetry,' Magistrate Lo said with satisfaction. He eyed the volumes piled up on the shelves against the side wall, the titles marked on neat red labels. The books were bristling with reading marks stuck among the leaves. Lo went to take a volume down, then thought better of it and asked curtly:

'The door-curtain back there leads to the bedroom, I suppose?'

As Meng nodded, Lo quickly pulled the curtain aside. The bedroom was somewhat larger than the library. Against the back wall stood a simple bedstead, the quilts turned back, and beside its head a small bedside table bearing a candle that had burnt out completely. A long bamboo flute was hanging from a nail on the wall. Opposite stood a dressing-table of carved ebony. The clothes-box of red pigskin had been pulled out from under the bed, its open lid revealing a mass of rumpled men's garments. In the back wall was a solid door, provided with a large bolt. A squat man in a blue gown was kneeling by the side of the dead man on the floor. Judge Dee saw over Lo's shoulder that the student had been a thin, bony man with a regular face adorned by a small moustache and chin-beard. His topknot had come loose; the hair was sticking to the pool of clotted blood on the floormat. His black cap, spattered with blood, was lying beside his head. He was clad in a white nightrobe, and he had soft felt shoes on his feet, the soles of which showed traces of dried mud. There was an ugly gash under his right ear.

The coroner came hastily to his feet and made a bow.

'The artery on the right side of his neck was cut by a savage blow, Your Honour. With a large knife or chopper, I'd say. About midnight, judging by the condition of the body. He was lying right here, on his face. I turned him over to verify whether there were other signs of violence, but I found none.'

Magistrate Lo muttered something, then devoted his attention to the tea-merchant, who had remained standing just inside the door. Twirling the points of his small moustache with thumb and forefinger, he gave Meng a thoughtful look. Judge Dee thought that Meng had a rather scholarly air: a long, sallow face, the thinness of which was stressed by the drooping moustache and ragged goatee.

'You also mentioned midnight, Mr Meng,' Lo suddenly said. 'Why?'

'It had struck me, sir,' the tea-merchant replied slowly, 'that although Mr Soong was dressed in his nightrobe, the bed had not been slept in. Now we know he kept late hours; there usually was a light in his window till midnight. Therefore I supposed that the murderer surprised Soong just when he was about to go to bed.'

Lo nodded. 'How did the murderer get inside, Mr Meng?'

The other sighed. Shaking his head, he replied:

'Mr Soong seems to have been a little absent-minded, Your Honour. The maids told my wife that he would often just sit and brood when they set the table for his meals, and did not reply when addressed. Last night he forgot to bolt the back door of this room, and also omitted to bar the garden gate. This way, please, Your Honour.'

The constable sitting on the ramshackle bamboo bench in the small garden sprang to attention. It crossed Judge Dee's mind that Lo had seen to it that his personnel were trained well: posting guards at all approaches to the scene of a crime was a precaution neglected by many more perfunctory magistrates. He bestowed a cursory look upon the shed that served as kitchen and washroom, then joined Lo and Meng who were going out through the narrow gate in the high garden wall. The headman of the constables followed them into the alley that ran between the forbidding garden walls of the houses in Mr Meng's lane and in the street running parallel to it. Pointing at the heaps of refuse that cluttered up the narrow passage, the tea-merchant remarked:

'Late at night vagabonds and ragpickers often roam about here, Your Honour, exploring these piles of rubbish. I warned Mr Soong always to keep the garden gate barred at night. Last night he must have gone out for a walk, and on his return forgotten to do so. Nor did he bolt the bedroom door, for when I found his dead body, it was standing ajar. The garden gate was closed but not barred. I'll show it to you, exactly as I found it.'

He took them back into the garden. A heavy wooden cross-bar was propped up against the garden wall, beside the gate. Mr Meng resumed:

'It's easy to reconstruct what happened, Your Honour. A ruffian passing through the alley noticed that the garden gate was ajar. He slipped into the garden and inside the house, assuming that the occupant was asleep. But Soong, who was just preparing for bed, spotted him. When the ruffian saw that Soong was all alone, he killed him on the spot. Then he ransacked the bedroom and the library. After he had discovered the cash-box, he took the money and left in the same way he had come.'

Magistrate Lo nodded slowly. 'Did Mr Soong usually keep a large sum of money in the cash-box?'

'That I couldn't tell you, sir. He paid one month's rent in advance, but he must have left at least travelling funds for his return journey to the capital. And there may have been some trinkets in his clothes-box.'

'We'll get the scoundrel soon enough, Excellency!' the headman remarked. 'Those ruffians always start spending freely as soon as they've made a good haul. Shall I order my men to make the round of the wine-houses and gambling-dens, sir?'

'Yes, do that, Headman. Let them also make discreet inquiries in the pawnshops. Place the body in a temporary coffin, and convey it to the mortuary in the tribunal. We must also inform the next of kin.' Magistrate Lo turned to the tea-merchant and asked, 'Soong will have had some friends or relatives here in this town, I suppose?'

'Apparently he hadn't, Your Honour. No one ever came to my house inquiring after him, and to the best of my know-ledge he never received visitors. Mr Soong was a serious, studious young man, kept himself very much to himself. I told him at our first meeting that he was always welcome for a cup of tea and a chat after dinner, but all through the past

19

two weeks he never availed himself of my invitation. That astonished me a bit, sir, for he was a polite, well-spoken youngster. As a common courtesy to one's host, one'd have expected that . . .'

'All right, Mr Meng. I'll tell my counsellor to write a letter to the Board of Education in the capital, asking them to inform Soong's family. Let's go back to the library.'

Lo offered Judge Dee the armchair at the desk. He himself pulled up a barrel-shaped seat to the bookshelves. He took a few volumes down and began to leaf through them.

'Aha!' he exclaimed. 'Your late mother was a lady of excellent literary taste, Mr Meng! She also read the minor poets, I see. Minor by the official standard, at least.' He shot a quick look at the judge and added with a smile, 'My friend Dee, being rather conservative, Mr Meng, probably won't agree. But personally I find those so-called minor poets more original than those who receive official recognition in the Imperial Catalogue.' He replaced the books, and took down a few others. While leafing through them he resumed without looking up, 'Since Mr Soong had no friends or relatives here in Chin-hwa, Mr Meng, how did he know that you wanted to rent your back-yard?'

'I happened to be visiting Your Honour's counsellor, Mr Kao, when Soong came to register two weeks ago, sir. Mr Kao was aware that I wanted to rent this section of my residence after my mother's death, and he kindly introduced me to Mr Soong. I took the student home with me, and showed him the yard. He was very pleased, said that it was exactly the kind of quiet lodging he had been looking for. He added that if his research in the old records would take more time than expected, he would like to prolong the tenancy. I was pleased too, for it isn't easy to . . .'

The tea-merchant broke off, for Lo didn't seem to be listening. He was absorbed in reading one of the paper slips tucked in the volume in his lap. The small magistrate looked up.

'Your mother's comments are very much to the point, Mr Meng. And she wrote a beautiful hand!'

'She practised calligraphy every morning, Your Honour, even after her eyesight deteriorated. And since my late father was also interested in poetry, they often discussed together the . . .'

'Excellent!' Lo exclaimed. 'Your house can boast of an elegant literary heritage, Mr Meng. You yourself continue that noble tradition, I trust?'

The tea-merchant smiled sadly.

'Unfortunately, Heaven decided to withhold its blessings for one generation, Your Honour. I myself have no talent for literature at all. But it seems that my son and daughter . . .'

'Very good! Well, Mr Meng, we shan't detain you any longer. You're doubtless eager to go to your shop. On the corner where our main thoroughfare is crossed by Temple Street, isn't it? Do you keep bitter tea from the south in stock? Yes? Good! I'll tell my housemaster to place an order with you. Best tea to drink after a heavy dinner. Shall do my utmost to get the ruffian who committed this brutal murder as soon as possible. Let you know at once when there's news. Good-bye, Mr Meng.'

The tea-merchant made his bow in front of the two magistrates, and the headman took him outside. When he was alone with Judge Dee, Lo slowly replaced the books on the shelf. He straightened the volumes carefully, then he folded his hands over his paunch. Rolling up his eyes, he exclaimed:

'Holy heaven, what terrible luck, elder brother! To be saddled with a complicated case of premeditated murder, just when I have to entertain such illustrious guests! And it'll take much hard work to solve this case, for the murderer was a clever devil. You agree that the cap was the only real mistake he made, don't you, Dee?'

21

IV

Judge Dee gave his colleague a sharp look. He leaned back in the armchair and, slowly caressing his long sidewhiskers, said:

'Yes, Lo, I fully agree with you that it was no murder for robbery committed by a vagrant ruffian. Even if we assume that Soong was so absent-minded as to have forgotten to bar and bolt both garden gate and bedroom door, a robber who saw a door standing ajar late at night would of course reconnoitre before entering the premises. He'd have made a peephole in the window-paper, for instance, and looked inside. Seeing Soong preparing for bed, he'd have waited an hour or so, and entered only after he had verified that the student was sound asleep.' As Lo nodded his round head vigorously, the judge went on, 'I am inclined to assume that when Soong had taken off his cap and upper robe, and had changed into his nightdress, preparing for bed, he heard a knock on the garden gate. He put on his cap again, and went outside to ask who it was.'

'Precisely!' Lo said. 'You'll also have noticed that there was a bit of dried mud on his house shoes.'

'I did. The visitor must have been someone known to Soong. The student took the bar from the gate, and led his visitor inside. Probably asked him to go on to the library, while he put on his upper robe. When Soong had his back turned, the visitor slew him from behind. I say from behind, because the wound is located under the victim's right ear. However that may be, I agree that leaving the cap where it had fallen on the floor was a bad mistake. For no man keeps his cap on his head while disrobing. The murderer ought to have cleansed the cap of bloodstains, and put it where it belonged, on the bed-table, beside the candle.'

'Absolutely!' Lo exclaimed. 'For the time being, however, we'll officially call it murder for robbery, so as not to alarm our man. As to his motive, I think it may well have been blackmail, Dee.'

Judge Dee sat up straight. 'Blackmail? What makes you think that, Lo?'

The small magistrate took a book down from the shelf, and opened it on a page marked by an inscribed slip of paper.

'Look, elder brother. Meng's mother was a tidy old lady, who kept her books neatly stacked. Now, however, the sequence of the volumes has become mixed up here and there. Further, every time she came upon a poem she particularly liked, she wrote her comments on a slip of paper like the one I have here, and inserted that slip into the book, exactly opposite the poem it referred to. However, leafing through a few volumes while talking with old Meng, I noticed that not a few slips had been inserted into the wrong places, and so carelessly that some had got false folds. Now I admit that the student might have been responsible for this. However, I also discovered recent smudges in the dust on the shelf behind the books. I think that the murderer ransacked the room only to make it appear as if a vagabond had been looking for money. And that the real object of his search was a document. Now, could you find a better place for concealing an important document than between the pages of a certain book, on the shelves of a well-stocked library? And if another fellow is then so keen on finding that document that he doesn't hesitate to commit a murder for it, one is inclined to think that the said document was of an incriminating nature; and then one thinks of blackmail.'

'You've made a very good point there, Lo.' Tapping the small pile of notepaper on the desk, the judge went on, 'These notes bear out your theory that the murderer was looking for a document. These are Soong's notes on his historical research. The first six pages are covered with his small, scholarly handwriting, the fifty or so that remain are still blank. You see that Soong was a methodical fellow, for he numbered each sheet. Yet the pile is askew, and on some of the blank sheets there are dusty fingermarks. Which indicates that the murderer carefully went through this pile. And what vagrant ruffian will ever bother to go through a bundle of manuscript notes?'

Lo got up with a deep sigh.

'Since the scoundrel had all night to search for the blasted paper, he probably found it too! But I am afraid we'll have to go over the place anyway, Dee. Just to make sure.'

Judge Dee got up too. Together they searched the library thoroughly. When the judge had sorted out the papers strewn on the floor and replaced them in the drawers, he remarked:

'All these documents are bills, receipts and so on of the Meng family. The only item that belonged to Soong is this small volume entitled *Tunes for the Straight Flute*, written in his hand, and marked with his seal. It's a complicated musical score unknown to me, consisting of abbreviated characters, as far as I can see. There are a dozen or so tunes, but the titles and the words have been omitted.'

Lo had been looking under the floormat. He righted himself and said:

'Yes, Soong played the flute. A long bamboo flute is hanging in his bedroom. Noticed it because I used to play the flute too, formerly.'

'Have you ever seen this system of notation?'

'No. I always played by ear,' Lo replied loftily. 'Well, we'd better go to work on the bedroom now, Dee. There's nothing here.'

The judge put the music book in his sleeve, and they went to the other room. The coroner was laboriously writing out his report on the autopsy, standing at the dressing-table, his portable writing-set at his elbow. Magistrate Lo took the flute that was hanging by a silk tassel from the nail in the wall. He shook back his sleeves with a determined gesture, and put the flute to his lips. But he succeeded only in producing a few disconcertingly shrill notes. Quickly lowering the flute, he said with a pained look:

'Used to play rather well, but I am out of practice. A good place to hide a document in, though. Tightly rolled up.' He peered into the flute, then shook his head disconsolately.

They went through the clothes-box, but the only papers they found were Soong's identity card and a few documents relating to his literary examinations. There was not one personal note or letter.

Shaking the dust from his robe, Judge Dee said:

'According to his landlord, Soong knew nobody here in your district. But Meng admits he hardly ever saw his lodger. We must question the maids who brought him his food, Lo.'

'That I must leave to you, elder brother! I really have to go home now. Have to pay my respects to my distinguished guests, you know. And my first, seventh and eighth wives told me this morning they want to consult me about purchases for the Moon Festival.'

'All right, I'll do the questioning.' While conducting his colleague to the door, the judge resumed, 'The feast'll be a big treat for your children, Lo. How many have you?'

Lo smiled broadly.

'Eleven boys and six girls,' he announced proudly. Then, however, his face fell. 'I've eight wives, you see. Quite a burden, Dee. Emotionally, I mean. Set out on my official career with only three wives, but you know how it goes. One contracts a friendship somewhere outside, then it seems so much simpler to put the lady in a pavilion within one's compound, and the next thing you know is that she's formally installed as a secondary wife! And it's sad to see how such a change in status will affect a woman's character, Dee. If I remember how nice and accommodating my eighth was when she was still dancing in the Sapphire Bower. . . .' Suddenly he smote his forehead. 'Holy heaven, I nearly forgot! I must drop in at the Sapphire Bower on my way back. To select the dancers for the dinner party tonight, you see. Always make it a point to choose them personally, feel it's my duty to see that my guests get only the best. Well, fortunately the Sapphire Bower is only a couple of streets from here.'

'Is it a house of assignation?'

Lo gave him a reproachful look.

'My dear fellow! Of course not! Call it a distribution centre of local talent. Or a training institute for the liberal arts.'

'Training institute or distribution centre,' Judge Dee said dryly, 'since the student Soong was all alone here, he may have paid a visit there late at night. Better inquire whether they remember a man answering the student's description, Lo.'

'Yes, I'll do that.' Suddenly the small magistrate chuckled. 'Must see also about a little surprise tonight. Specially for you, Dee!'

'You'll do nothing of the sort!' the judge told him acidly. 'I must say I fail to understand how you can be thinking of frolicking with women while this murder case . . .'

Lo raised his hand.

'You have me all wrong, elder brother! My surprise concerns an intriguing judicial problem.'

'Oh yes. I . . . I see,' the judge said contritely. He resumed quickly, 'Anyway, I think we can do without another judicial problem, Lo. Soong's murder is intriguing enough! If that unfortunate student had been a local citizen, we'd at least know where to look for clues. But since Soong arrived here out of the blue, so to speak, I fear that . . .'

'You know that I never mix business with pleasure, Dee,'

Lo said primly. 'The brutal murder of Soong is official business. My surprise for you, on the other hand, is a purely theoretical problem, for its legal consequences concern neither of us. You'll meet the main person at dinner tonight, Dee! Tantalizing puzzle. It'll tickle you no end!'

Judge Dee shot his colleague a suspicious look. Then he said briskly, 'Please order the steward to bring the maid who used to serve Soong here, Lo. And send a palankeen to fetch me, will you?'

As Magistrate Lo took the path across the orchard, two guards carrying a bamboo stretcher made way for him. Judge Dee took them to the bedroom. While the guards rolled the dead body in a reed mat and placed it on the stretcher, the judge read the official report the coroner had handed him. Stuffing it into his sleeve, he said:

'You state here only that the mortal blow was inflicted by a sharp instrument. I noticed it wasn't a clean-cut wound—a jagged gash, rather. What about a chisel or a file, or some other carpenter's tool?'

The coroner pursed his lips.

'Quite possible, sir. Since the murder weapon was not found, I didn't like to commit myself.'

'I see. You may leave now, coroner. I'll hand your report to the magistrate.'

An elderly man with a pronounced stoop herded two girls inside. Both wore simple blue gowns with black sashes round their waists. The younger was small and rather plain-looking, but the other had a round, attractive face, and her carriage showed she was well aware of her good figure. Judge Dee motioned them to follow him to the library. When he had let himself down into the armchair again, the old steward pushed the small girl to the front and said with a bow:

'This is Peony, sir. She used to serve Soong his noon rice, clean up and make the bed. The other is called Aster. She brought him his evening meals.'

27

'Well, Peony,' the judge addressed the plain girl kindly, 'Mr Soong must have given you quite a lot of extra work. Especially when he had company.'

'Oh no, sir, Mr Soong never had any visitors. And I didn't mind a little extra work, sir, for it's an easy household, since the Old Lady died. There's only the master and the first and second mistress, and their son and daughter. Very kind persons, all of them, sir. And Mr Soong also was a kind gentleman. Gave me a tip for doing his laundry.'

'He often engaged you in small talk, I suppose?'

'Only good morning and so on, sir. He was a scholarly gentleman, sir. Terrible to think that now he . . .'

'Thank you. Take Peony outside, Steward.' When he was alone with the elder girl, the judge resumed, 'Peony is a little country lass, Aster. You look like a girl about town who knows what's what, and . . .' He had expected a smile, but she just stared fixedly at him, a glint of fear in her wide eyes. Suddenly she asked:

'Is it true what the steward said, sir? That his throat was bitten through?'

The judge raised his eyebrows.

'Bitten through, you say? What nonsense is this? Mr Soong's neck had been cut with a . . .' He broke off in mid-sentence, remembering the jagged gash. 'Speak up!' he resumed testily. 'What do you mean by bitten through?'

Looking down at her tightly clasped hands, she said in a surly voice:

'Mr Soong had a girl friend. I am going steady with the head-waiter in the large tea-house in the next street, and the other night when we stood talking on the corner of the back alley, we saw Mr Soong slip outside, stealthy-like. All dressed up in black.'

'Did you see him meet his girl there?'

'No, sir. But a couple of days ago he asked me whether the silver shop behind the Temple of Confucius still sells those hairpins with round filigree knobs. He wanted a present for his girl, of course. And she . . . she killed him.'

Judge Dee gave her an uncertain look.

'What exactly do you mean?' he asked quietly.

'She was a fox, sir! A fox posing as a beautiful young girl, so as to bewitch him. And when he was completely in her power, she bit his throat.' Seeing Judge Dee's contemptuous smile, she went on quickly, 'He was under a spell, sir, I swear it! And he knew it, for he asked me once whether there were many foxes here, and where they . . .'

'A level-headed young woman like you,' the judge interrupted, 'ought to know better than to believe those silly stories about fox-magic. Foxes are just nice, clever animals that harm nobody.'

'The people here don't think so, sir,' she said stubbornly. 'I tell you that he was bewitched by a female fox. You should've heard those weird tunes he used to play on his flute at night! That strange music carried all across the orchard. I could hear it when I was combing my master's daughter's hair.'

'As I passed the family quarters, I saw a handsome young girl looking through the window. That was Mr Meng's daughter, I suppose?'

'Must've been her, sir. Handsome is as handsome does, and she's an open-handed, nice girl. Only sixteen, but very good at making poetry, people say.'

'To come back to your boy friend, Aster. Has Mr Soong ever visited the tea-house where he works? It's quite near, you said.'

'No, sir. He's never seen the student anywhere. And he knows all the tea- and wine-houses in this neighbourhood— too well! Please don't tell the master about my boy friend, sir. The master is very old-fashioned, and . . .'

'Don't worry, Aster, I shan't.' The judge rose. 'Thanks very much.'

Outside he told the steward to take him to the main gate, where a small litter stood waiting.

As he was carried back to the tribunal, the judge reflected that the student's murder would probably not be solved before his departure for Poo-yang. It had all the makings of a vexing, time-consuming case. Well, Magistrate Lo would know how to deal with it. His colleague had handled the investigation on the spot in a businesslike manner, and he was a shrewd observer. Doubtless he also would have realized that this might after all turn out to be an inside case. The tea-merchant had seemed over-eager to convince them that a vagrant ruffian from outside had committed the crime. There were all kinds of interesting possibilities.

He pulled the six pages of the student's notes from his sleeve, and read them through carefully. Then he leaned back, pensively tugging at his moustache. The notes were to the point. Names of rebel leaders were listed that apparently were not mentioned in the official history, and data on the economic situation in the district at the time of the peasant revolt, two hundred years ago. Yet it seemed but a meagre result, if one remembered that Soong had spent every afternoon in the chancery archives during the past two weeks. The judge decided he would draw Lo's attention to the possibility that Soong's historical research had been only a pretext, and that he had come to Chin-hwa for quite a different reason.

It was curious that the superstition about fox-magic was so strong in this district. Popular belief all over the country credited the fox with supernatural powers, and the storytellers on the market loved to expand on old tales of foxes changing themselves into beautiful young girls to bewitch young men, or into old gentlemen of venerable appearance who led unsuspecting young girls astray. But classical literature, on the contrary, stated that the fox had mystic powers over malicious spirits. Therefore one would often find in old palaces and public offices a small shrine dedicated to the fox spirit, which was supposed to ward off evil, and to protect especially the official seals, the emblems of authority. He thought he had seen such a small shrine in his colleague's residence.

He wondered uneasily what surprise his colleague had in store for him at dinner, for he profoundly distrusted Lo's particular kind of impish humour. Heaven only knew what mischief he was up to now! Lo had suggested that one of his guests was involved in a judicial problem. The person concerned could hardly be the Academician or the Court Poet, both high-ranking officials and famous men of letters, certainly capable of dealing effectively with all their personal problems, judicial or not! It had to be that mysterious sexton who had got himself into trouble. Well, he would know soon enough. The judge closed his eyes.

V

Walking along the broad corridor of the chancery facing Lo's residence, Judge Dee bestowed a casual look upon the dozen or so clerks who were busily wielding their writing-brushes at high desks, piled with dossiers and papers. Since the tribunal is the administrative centre of the entire district, it is not only the seat of criminal jurisdiction, but also the registration office of births, marriages and deaths, and of sales and purchases of landed property; moreover, the tribunal is responsible for the collection of taxes, including land tax. When the judge passed the lattice door of the hall at the end of the corridor, he saw through the open woodwork the counsellor, bent over his desk. He knew Kao only by sight. On the impulse of the moment he pushed the door open and went into the scrupulously clean office.

Kao looked up and quickly got to his feet.

'Please be seated, Excellency! Can I offer you a cup of tea?'

'Don't trouble, Mr Kao. I won't sit down, for I am expected in the residence. Has Magistrate Lo told you the result of our visit to the scene of Soong's murder?'

'My chief was in a hurry to see his guests, sir. He just dropped in and ordered me to inform the Board of Education in the capital that Soong had been murdered, and ask them to apprise the next of kin.' Handing the judge a draft, he added, 'I also asked the Board to ascertain the family's wishes regarding the burial.'

'Very good, Mr Kao. You'd better add a request for information regarding the student's background. Just to complete the record.' Returning the draft to Kao, he resumed, 'Mr Meng told us that you had introduced Soong to him. Do you know the tea-merchant well?'

'Yes indeed, sir. When I was transferred here five years ago from the Prefect's office, I made Mr Meng's acquaintance in the local chess club. Now we meet there every week for a game. I came to know him as a man of elevated character, sir. Rather conservative, but by no means an old fogey. And a strong chess player!'

'Being an old-fashioned gentleman, Mr Meng keeps his household in proper order, I suppose? Never any rumours about clandestine relations or . . .'

'Never, sir! A model household, I'd call it! I paid a courtesy call on Meng, and had the honour to be presented to the Old Lady, who was then still alive. Locally she was well known as a poetess, sir. And Mr Meng's son is an intelligent youngster, he's only fourteen and already in the highest form of the District School.'

'Yes, Mr Meng made a most favourable impression on me. Well, thanks for your information, Mr Kao.'

The counsellor conducted Judge Dee all the way to the monumental entrance gate of Magistrate Lo's private residence. Just as the judge was about to enter, a broad-shouldered officer came outside. He wore the black, red-bordered tunic of the Prefecture, the long red tassels on his iron helmet indicating that he was a sergeant of the guard. A broadsword was strapped to his back. The judge went to ask him whether he had brought a message from the Prefect, but desisted when he saw the round bronze plaque hanging on a chain from the sergeant's neck. This was the token that he was on special duty, conveying a criminal to the capital. The tall officer hurriedly crossed the yard to overtake Counsellor Kao. Vaguely Judge Dee wondered what important criminal was being escorted through Chin-hwa.

He went to the right wing of the first courtyard, and opened the narrow, red-lacquered door that gave access to the courtyard that Magistrate Lo had placed at his disposal. It was small, but a unity in itself, the high surrounding walls giving it a pleasant atmosphere of quiet privacy. In front of his spacious bed-sitting-room ran a gallery, two steps leading down into the square yard, paved with coloured tiles. In the centre was a small goldfish pond, with a rockery behind it. The judge paused for a moment on the gallery, under the red-lacquered beams of the overhanging eaves, and admired the charming scene. From the crevices of the rockery, covered with moss, grew tufts of slender bamboos, and a small shrub of shining red berries. Over the garden wall he could see the tall maple trees of the park surrounding the residence. A breeze rustled their foliage, aglow with the rich colours of autumn: red, brown and yellow. He estimated it was about four o'clock.

The judge turned round, pushed the sliding-doors of red-lacquered lattice-work open and went inside, making straight for the tea-basket on the side-table, for he was very thirsty. To his disappointment he found it empty. Well, it didn't matter, for presently his two hosts would offer him tea. His immediate problem was whether or not to change. Both the Academician and the Court Poet were senior in age and rank, so properly speaking he ought to visit them as he was, in full ceremonial dress. On the other hand, neither of the two was occupying an official post at the moment. The Academician had gone into retirement a year ago, and Chang had resigned his position at Court, in order to devote himself entirely to editing a complete edition of his poetic oeuvre. If the judge visited them in his ceremonial dress, they might take that as an impertinence, as an attempt to stress that he, the judge, was an official in function whereas they were not. Heaving a sigh, he thought of the old proverb, 'It's safer to beard a tiger in its lair than to approach a high official'. Finally he decided upon a long-sleeved violet gown with a broad black sash, and a high square cap of black gauze. He hoped that this dignified but modest attire would meet with approval, and went outside.

JUDGE DEE VISITS THE ACADEMICIAN

The judge had noticed already that although the buildings of the front courtyard, including his own quarters, consisted of only one storey, those of the other courtyards further on had second floors, lined with broad balconies. Now he saw on the balcony of the tall building in the back of the main courtyard many boy servants and maids coming and going. Evidently they were making preparations for the dinner party there that night. He estimated that his colleague's household personnel must count at least a hundred persons, and shuddered when he calculated the cost involved in maintaining such a palatial residence.

He hailed a servant, who informed him that Magistrate Lo had ceded his own library to the Academician, in the left wing of the second court, and assigned to the Court Poet the corner apartment of the right wing. The judge ordered the boy to take him to the library first. When he had knocked on the beautifully carved door panel, a deep voice called, 'Come in!'

The judge saw at a glance that Lo had made his library into an attractive and comfortable retreat. It was a spacious, lofty room with broad lattice windows showing intricate geometrical designs that stood out against the spotless paper panes. Two walls were lined with well-stocked bookshelves, here and there interrupted by niches displaying a few choice antique bowls and vases. The furniture consisted of solid pieces of carved blackwood, the tops of the tables were of coloured marble, the chairs cushioned with red silk. Large vases mounted on ebony stands and filled with white and yellow chrysanthemums flanked the massive bench in front of the bookshelves. There a heavily-built, broad-shouldered man sat reading a book. He put the volume down and gave Judge Dee a curious look, raising one of his thick, tufted eyebrows. He wore an ample, sapphire-blue gown, open at the neck, and a black silk cap, decorated in front by a round plaque of translucent green jade. The long ends of the sash round his waist trailed down on to the floor. His broad, heavy-jowled face was framed by short sidewhiskers and a neatly trimmed ring beard, as was then the fashion at the Imperial Court. The judge knew that the Academician was getting on for sixty, but his beard and whiskers were still jet black.

Judge Dee stepped up to him, made a low bow, and handed him his red visiting-card respectfully, with both hands. The Academician cast a cursory glance at it. Putting the card in his capacious sleeve, he spoke in his rumbling voice:

'So you are Dee from Poo-yang. Yes, young Lo told me that you were staying here too. Nice place, better than that cramped room in the government hostel I passed the night in. Glad to meet you, Dee. You did a good job in cleaning up that temple in Poo-yang. Made you a lot of enemies at Court, but also friends. All good men have both enemies and friends, Dee. No use trying to be everybody's friend, gets you nowhere.' He rose and walked over to the writing-desk. Sitting down in the armchair, he pointed at a low footstool. 'Well, take that seat opposite me!'

The judge sat down and began politely:

'This person has long been looking forward eagerly to an opportunity for paying his respects to Your Excellency. Now that . . .'

The Academician waved a large, shapely hand.

'Let's skip all that, shall we? We are not at Court here. Just an informal gathering of amateur poets. You write poetry too, don't you, Dee?'

He fixed the judge with his large eyes, where the black stood out clearly against the white.

'Hardly, sir,' the judge replied diffidently. 'I had to learn the rules of prosody, of course, when I was a student. And I have read our famous classical anthologies, so ably edited by you, sir. But I have written only one poem myself.'

'The fame of many an illustrious man rests just on one poem, Dee!' He pulled the large teapot of blue porcelain towards him. 'You've had your tea already, of course, Dee.' As the Academician poured himself a cup, Judge Dee got a whiff of delicate jasmine. After having taken a few sips, his host resumed, 'Well, tell me what your poem was about.'

Clearing his dry throat, the judge replied:

'It was a didactic poem, sir, on the importance of agriculture. I tried to compress seasonal directions for the farmers in a hundred rhymed stanzas.'

The Academician shot him a quizzical look.

'You did, did you? Why did you choose that, eh . . . rather peculiar theme?'

'Because I hoped that such directions if put into verse, with rhythm and rhyme, might be remembered more easily by simple country folk, sir.'

The other smiled.

'Most people would consider that a foolish answer, Dee. Not I. Poetry is indeed easy to remember. Not only because of the rhyme, but chiefly because it responds to the beat of our blood, and to the rhythm of our respiration. Rhythm is the bone-structure of all good poetry, and of prose too. Recite a few couplets from your poem, Dee!'

The judge shifted uncomfortably in his seat.

'To tell you the truth, sir, I wrote it more than ten years ago. I am afraid I don't recall a single couplet, at the moment. But I'll send you a copy, if I may, for . . .'

'Don't trouble, Dee! Let me tell you frankly that it must have been bad poetry. If there had been a few good lines in it, you'd never have forgotten those. Tell me, did you ever read the "Imperial Rescript to the Officers and Men of the Seventh Army"?'

'I know it by heart, sir!' the judge exclaimed. 'That inspiring message to a retreating army turned the tide of battle, sir! Those stately opening lines . . .'

'Exactly, Dee! You'll never forget that text, because it was good prose, the rhythm of which pulsated in the blood of every man at arms, from the generals to the foot-soldiers.

Therefore people still recite it now, all over our Empire. I drafted it for His Majesty, by the way. Well, Dee, you must give me your views on local administration. I always enjoy talking with young officials, you know. Always consider it one of the many drawbacks of a high position at Court that we get out of touch with provincial officials. And I am especially interested in district problems, Dee. It's the lowest administrative level, of course, but of basic importance.' He slowly emptied his cup under the envious eyes of Judge Dee, carefully wiped his moustache and resumed with a reminiscent smile:

'I started as a district magistrate myself, you know! Served in only one post, though, for then I wrote my memorial on judicial reform, and I was promoted to Prefect in the south, then transferred here to this very region! Hectic times those were, when the Ninth Prince rebelled, twenty years ago. And now we are in his old mansion! Yes, time flies, Dee. Well, then I published my critical notes on the Classics, and I was appointed Reader in the Imperial Academy. Was allowed to accompany His Majesty on the August Inspection Tour of the western regions. On that journey I composed my "Odes on the Szuchuan Mountains". Still consider that my best poetry, Dee.' He loosened the collar of his robe, baring his thick, muscular neck. The judge remembered that the Academician had also been a well-known wrestler and swordsman in his younger years. His host took up the book that was lying open on the desk.

'Found this on Lo's shelves, Counsellor Hwang's collected poems on Szuchuan scenery. Visited the same places as I did. Very interesting to compare our impressions. This verse is quite good, but . . .' He bent over the page, then shook his head. 'No, this metaphor doesn't ring quite true . . .' Suddenly remembering his guest he looked up and said with a smile, 'Shouldn't bother you with all this, Dee! You've doubtless many things to attend to before dinner.'

Judge Dee rose. The Academician got up too, and despite his guest's protests insisted on seeing him to the door.

'Thoroughly enjoyed our talk, Dee! Always keen on hearing the views of young officials. Makes one look at things with a fresh eye, so to speak. See you tonight!'

Judge Dee walked hurriedly over to the right wing, for his parched throat was making him really long for a cup of tea. There were many doors along the open gallery, but he looked in vain for a servant to tell him which was the Court Poet's room. Then his eye fell on a thin man in a faded grey robe who was feeding the goldfish in the granite basin at the end of the gallery. He wore a flat black cap with a thin red seam. Apparently one of his colleague's stewards. The judge walked up to him and asked:

'Could you tell me where I can find the Honourable Chang Lan-po?'

The other raised his head and looked him up and down with his heavy-lidded, strangely still eyes. Then a shy smile curved his lips, thin above the sparse, greying chinbeard. He said in a colourless voice:

'He is here. I am Chang Lan-po, as a matter of fact.'

'A thousand pardons, sir!' Judge Dee quickly took his visiting-card from his sleeve and offered it to the poet with a low bow. 'I came to pay you my respects, sir.'

The poet stared absent-mindedly at the card, holding it in his thin, blue-veined hand. 'Most considerate of you, Dee,' he said mechanically. Pointing at the basin, he resumed in a more animated voice, 'Look at that small fish under the water-weeds in the corner! Do you notice the perplexed look in its large, bulging eyes? It forcibly reminds me of ourselves . . . bewildered observers.' Then he lifted his hooded eyes. 'Excuse me, please. Raising goldfish is one of my hobbies, you see. Makes me forget my manners. How long have you been staying here, Dee?'

'I arrived the day before yesterday, sir.'

'Oh yes, the Prefect held a conference of magistrates here, I heard. I do hope you are enjoying your stay in Chin-hwa, Dee. I am a native of this district, you know.'

'It's a beautiful city, sir. And I feel most honoured that now I have an opportunity of meeting its most distinguished and brilliant . . .'

The poet shook his head.

'No, not brilliant, Dee. Not any more, unfortunately.' He put the small ivory box with goldfish food back in his sleeve. 'I apologize, Dee, but I feel a bit out of sorts today. The visit to my ancestral shrine made me dwell on the past . . .' He broke off and darted a shy glance at his visitor. 'Tonight, at dinner, I'll brighten up a little. Have to, for my friend the Academician always draws me into involved literary arguments. He has a truly encyclopaedic knowledge of literature, Dee, and an unrivalled command of the language. A bit high and mighty, but . . .' Suddenly he asked anxiously, 'You have visited him before coming to me, I hope?'

'I did, sir.'

'Very good. I must warn you that despite his bohemian airs, Shao is very conscious of his exalted position, and quick to take offence. I am sure you'll enjoy tonight's gathering, Dee. With Sexton Loo present, there won't be a dull moment! And it's a rare privilege to meet our famous colleague who has suddenly become so notorious now. We must . . .' He clapped his hand to his mouth. 'Nearly spoke out of turn there! Our mutual friend Lo made me promise I wouldn't tell you! Lo is fond of his little surprises, as you doubtless know.' He passed his hand over his face. 'Well, excuse me for not asking you inside for a cup of tea. I am really rather tired, Dee, ought to take a nap before dinner. I didn't sleep well last night. The hostel was so noisy . . .'

'Of course, sir. I quite understand!' The judge took his leave with a bow, his hands respectfully folded in his long sleeves.

While walking down the gallery he decided that now that he had paid his official calls, he must try to get hold of Lo to report what he had learned from the maid in the tea-merchant's house. And to get a cup of tea at long last!

VI

Judge Dee went to the counsellor's office, and asked Kao to inquire whether Magistrate Lo could receive him. The counsellor came back after only a few minutes.

'My master'll be glad to see you, sir. In his private office back of here.' Giving the judge a shy look, he added, 'I do hope you'll be able to cheer him up a little, sir!'

The small magistrate was sitting in a cushioned armchair behind a colossal writing-desk of polished ebony, staring moodily at the pile of documents in front of him. When he saw the judge he jumped up and shouted:

'All those self-styled experts on the calendar in our Ministry of Rites should get the sack, Dee. At once! They don't know their job. The fools marked today as a particularly lucky day! And since noon just about everything has been going wrong!' He let himself down into his chair again, angrily puffing out his round cheeks.

Judge Dee took the armchair beside the desk and poured himself a cup of tea from the padded basket. After he had greedily emptied it, he refilled the cup, then leaned back with a satisfied sigh and listened silently to his colleague's tale of woe.

'First we got that nasty murder of student Soong, just after a copious repast, and that ruined my digestion. Then the lady in charge of the Sapphire Bower informed me that their best dancer is ill. I'll have to make do for tonight with two second-rate ones, and for the main number I could only get a wench called Small Phoenix, and I didn't like her looks. Silly face, and as thin as a beanpole! Push that tea-basket over to me, will you?' He refilled Judge Dee's cup and his own, took a sip and resumed, 'Finally, that nice surprise I had thought up

43

for you came to nothing. The Academician and the Court Poet will be terribly disappointed too. And it means we'll be five at dinner. Besides you and me, Shao, Chang and Sexton Loo. An odd number at table means bad luck. And the calendar said specifically that this would be a lucky day. Pah!' He set his cup down hard and asked peevishly, 'Well, what's the news about our murder case? The headman dropped in a few moments ago and reported that his men haven't heard anything about a local ruffian being free with his money. Just as we had already expected.'

The judge emptied his third cup.

'According to one of the maids who used to serve Soong, he had visited this city before. And apparently he had a girl friend here.'

Lo sat up. 'The devil he had! But not in the Sapphire Bower, at any rate. I described him to the girls, and they had never set eyes on him.'

'Second,' Judge Dee continued, 'I suspect that Soong came here for a special reason which he wanted to keep secret, and that his historical research was just a pretext.' He took the student's notes from his sleeve and handed them to Lo. 'These six pages are all the notes he made during those two weeks!'

Lo glanced through the notes. When he nodded, the judge continued:

'Every afternoon Soong visited your archives, to keep up appearances. In the night he went out about his real business. The maid saw him slip outside, in a dark gown, and in a stealthy manner.'

'Not a single clue as to where he went or what he did, Dee?'

'No. The maid knows a waiter in a tea-house near-by who seems to be rather a gay blade, and he never saw Soong anywhere in that neighbourhood.' He cleared his throat. 'That maid firmly believes in fox-magic, you know. Maintains that Soong's girl was in fact a fox, and murdered him!'

'Oh yes, the fox plays an important role in local folklore, Dee. We have a fox shrine in the residence, it's supposed to guard the premises. And there's a big one on a piece of wasteland, near the south city gate. Place is haunted, people say. Well, we'd better keep the supernatural out of this, Dee! Case is sufficiently difficult as it is!'

'I couldn't agree more, Lo. You also reckon with the possibility that it was an inside affair, don't you?'

'Yes, indeed. Meng's reputation is of the best, but that doesn't mean a thing, of course. Might have known Soong when the student visited this district formerly. And Meng did quite a bit of detective work all on his own, Dee, just after his discovery of the dead body. And was very eager to pass his theory on to us. Easiest thing for Meng to walk round the block, and knock on his own garden door! And I don't like this business about Soong having a girl friend. Don't like it at all. Girls mean trouble.' He heaved a sigh. 'Anyway, there are no sessions of the tribunal tomorrow, because of the Mid-autumn Festival. That gives us a little respite, at least.'

Lo poured himself another cup, and sank into a morose silence.

Judge Dee looked at him expectantly, waiting for Lo to explain how he was planning to proceed with the investigation. If this case had happened in Poo-yang, he would at once have ordered his three lieutenants, Ma Joong, Chiao Tai and Tao Gan, to make inquiries in the tea-merchant's neighbourhood, about Meng himself, his family and his lodger. It was amazing how much information experienced officers could collect in vegetable, fish and butcher shops. Not to forget the cheap street-stalls where the chairbearers and coolies gather. As his colleague remained silent, Judge Dee said:

'We can't do anything about this case ourselves tonight, because of the dinner. Did you send out members of your staff to make further inquiries?'

'No, Dee, I employ the staff of the tribunal for routine mat-

45

ters only. All confidential inquiries are organized by my old housemaster.' Seeing Judge Dee's astonished face, he went on quickly, 'The old geezer was born and bred here, you see, knows the city like the palm of his hand. He has three distant relatives, slick fellows who work as clerks in a pawnshop, at a silversmith's, and in a popular restaurant in the market. I pay them a generous salary out of my own pocket, for acting as my stool pigeons and secret inquiry agents. System works quite well. Enables me to keep a check on my counsellor and the rest of the tribunal personnel too.'

The judge nodded slowly. He himself relied unreservedly on his old adviser Hoong and his three lieutenants. But every magistrate was free to work in his own way, and Lo's system didn't seem too bad. Especially since during his previous visit to Chin-hwa he had come to know Lo's housemaster as a crafty old rascal. 'Have you told your housemaster to . . .' he began. Then there was a knock on the door. The headman came in and reported:

'A Miss Yoo-lan asks for an audience, Excellency.'

Lo's face lit up in a broad smile. He thumped his fist on the desk and exclaimed, 'Must mean she's reconsidered! A lucky day after all, maybe! Show her in, my man! At once!' Rubbing his hands, he told Judge Dee, 'To all appearances my little surprise for you is coming off, elder brother!'

The judge raised his eyebrows.

'Yoo-lan? Who is that?'

'My dear fellow! Do you mean to say that you, one of our greatest experts on crime, haven't yet heard about the maid's murder, in the White Heron Monastery?'

Judge Dee sat up with a gasp.

'Merciful heaven, Lo! You can't mean the case of that awful Taoist nun who whipped her maidservant to death?'

Lo nodded happily.

'The very same woman, Dee! The great Yoo-lan. Courtesan, poetess, Taoist nun, famous . . .'

The judge had grown red in the face.

'A despicable murderess!' he shouted angrily.

The magistrate raised his podgy hand.

'Steady, Dee, steady, please! In the first place, may I remind you that it's the consensus of opinion in scholarly circles that she has been falsely accused? Her case was heard in the District, Prefectural and Provincial Courts, in that order, and none of them could reach a verdict. That's why she is now being conveyed to the capital, where she'll be judged by the Metropolitan Court. Second, she is without doubt the most accomplished woman writer of the Empire. Both the Academician and the Court Poet know her well, and they were delighted when I told them I had ordered her escort to let her stay two days in my residence.' He paused, and plucked at his moustache. 'However, when I went to see her this afternoon, in the inn behind the Sapphire Bower where she's staying with her armed escort, she refused my invitation point-blank. Said she didn't want to meet old friends until her innocence had been proved beyond all doubt. Imagine my mortification, Dee! I had hoped to give you the opportunity of discussing the most sensational murder case of the year with the accused herself. Offer you a stimulating puzzle that is baffling three judicial inquiries. Present it to you on a platter, so to speak! I know you aren't exactly an ardent student of poetry, Dee, and I wanted you to have an interesting time here all the same!'

Judge Dee smoothed his long beard, groping in his mind for the details of the murder case. Then he said with a smile:

'I do appreciate your kind thought, Lo. But I still hope she won't come. For as regards puzzles, we have . . .'

The door opened. The headman ushered inside a tall woman clad in a black gown and jacket. Ignoring Judge Dee, she strode up to the desk and told Lo in a deep, melodious voice:

'I want to tell you that I have reconsidered, Magistrate. I accept your kind invitation.'

47

'Excellent, my dear lady, excellent! Shao and Chang are both looking forward to meeting you again. Sexton Loo is here too, you know. And let me introduce to you another admirer of yours! This is my friend Dee, the magistrate of our neighbour-district, Poo-yang. I present the great Yoo-lan to you, Dee!'

She gave the judge a cursory look from her vivacious, long-lashed eyes, and made a perfunctory bow. When the judge had acknowledged the greeting by inclining his head, she turned her attention to the small magistrate, who was setting out on a detailed description of the courtyard he had prepared for her, next door to his own women's quarters, at the back of his residence.

Judge Dee put her age at about thirty. Formerly she must have been remarkably beautiful. She still had a regular, expressive face, but there were heavy pouches under her eyes, a deep furrow between her long, curved eyebrows, and thin lines by the side of her full mouth, very red in her pallid face, devoid of rouge and powder. Her hair was done up in a high coiffure of three jet-black coils, held in place by two simple ivory needles. The severe black dress accentuated her broad hips, slender waist and rather too heavy bosom. When she bent over the desk to pour herself a cup of tea, he noticed her white, sensitive hands, unadorned by rings or bracelets.

'A thousand thanks for all your trouble,' she cut short her host's harangue. A soft smile lighting up her face, she continued, 'And ten thousand thanks for showing me that I still have friends! I was beginning to think I had none left, during the past few weeks. I gather there will be a dinner tonight?'

'Certainly, but just a small affair, in my residence. To-morrow night we shall all go to the Emerald Cliff, and celebrate the Mid-autumn Festival there together!'

'That sounds most attractive, Magistrate. Especially after six weeks spent in various prisons. They treated me well, I must say, but still . . . Well, tell your headman to take me to your residence and introduce me to the matron of your women's quarters. I must take a good rest, and change before dinner. Even a woman past her prime likes to look her best on such occasions.'

'Of course, my dear!' Lo exclaimed. 'Take all the time you want! We'll start dinner late, and go on till deep into the night, in the style of the ancients!' As he clapped his hands for the headman, the poetess said:

'Oh, yes, I brought Small Phoenix with me. She wanted to have a look at the hall where she's supposed to dance tonight. You made a good choice there, Magistrate.' And to the headman who came in, 'Bring the young woman here!'

A slender girl of about eighteen stepped inside and dropped a curtsey. She was dressed in a plain dark-blue gown, a red sash wound tightly round her wasp-like waist. Magistrate Lo surveyed her critically, a frown creasing his thin eyebrows.

'Ah, yes. Ha hm,' he said vaguely. 'Well, my girl, I don't think you'll find anything wrong with my hall.'

'Don't try to be nasty, Magistrate!' the poetess intervened curtly. 'She's very serious about her art, and wants to adapt her dances to the floor-space available. Tonight she's going to dance to that enchanting tune "A Phoenix among Purple Clouds". That's her most popular number. The title goes well with her name too! Come on, don't be shy, dear! Always remember that a handsome young girl needn't be afraid of any gentleman, high official or not.'

The dancer looked up. Judge Dee was struck by her curious still face. The long, pointed nose and the large, lacklustre eyes with a pronounced upward slant gave it a mask-like quality. Her hair was drawn back tightly from her smooth high brow, and gathered in a simple coil at the nape of her long, thin neck. She had angular shoulders and thin, long arms. There was a strange, sexless aura about her. The judge could well imagine that his colleague was not greatly impressed, for he knew that Lo went for flamboyant women, with obvious and very feminine charms.

'This person regrets her slender abilities,' the dancer said in a voice so low as to be hardly audible. 'It is too great an honour to be allowed to dance before such distinguished company.'

The poetess patted her lightly on the shoulder.

'That'll do, dear. I'll see you tonight at dinner, gentlemen!'

Again she made a perfunctory bow and went out with her quick, long stride, followed by the shy dancer.

Magistrate Lo raised both his hands and cried out:

'That woman had absolutely everything! Great beauty, extraordinary talent, and a forceful personality. To think that a cruel fate ordained that I should meet her ten years too late!' Sadly shaking his head, he pulled a drawer out and took from it a bulky dossier. He resumed briskly, 'I collected copies of all relevant documents concerning the murder for you, Dee. Thought you'd like to know all the circumstances of the White Heron murder case. Added a brief note on her career too, for your orientation. Here, you had better have a look at these papers before dinner.'

The judge was touched. His colleague had really gone to a great deal of trouble just to see that he, his guest, wouldn't be bored. He said gratefully:

'That's most thoughtful of you, Lo! You are really a perfect host!'

'Don't mention it, elder brother! No trouble at all!' He darted a quick look at the judge, and resumed, a little contritely, 'Ahem, must confess that I have also what might be described as an ulterior motive, Dee. Fact is that I have been planning for some time to publish an annotated edition of Yoo-lan's complete poetical oeuvre, you see. Drafted the preface already. A murder conviction would wreck the plan, of course. Hoped you'd help her to draw up a really convincing plea of innocence, elder brother. You being such a past master in the drafting of legal documents and so forth. See what I mean?'

'I do indeed,' Judge Dee replied stiffly. Giving his colleague a frosty look, he rose and tucked the dossier under his arm. 'Well, I'd better set to work at once.'

VII

Entering the main gate of the residence, Judge Dee halted in his steps and cast an astonished look at the disreputable figure standing at the door of his own quarters. It was a short, obese man in an old, patched monk's habit, his round, shaven head bare. He wore large, worn-out straw sandals on his feet. Wondering how a beggar could have gained entrance to the residence, the judge stepped up to him and asked curtly:

'What do you want here?'

The other turned round. Fixing the judge with his large, protruding eyes, he replied gruffly:

'Ha, Magistrate Dee! Went to look in on you for a moment or two, but there was no answer to my knocking.' His voice was hoarse, but he spoke like an educated man, and with authority. Suddenly Judge Dee understood.

'Glad to meet you, Sexton Loo. Magistrate Lo told me that . . .'

'Decide later whether you're glad to have met me or not, Dee!' the sexton interrupted. He was staring past the judge with his unblinking eyes. Involuntarily the judge looked over his shoulder. The courtyard was deserted.

'No, you can't see them, Judge. Not yet. Don't let it worry you. The dead are always with us. Everywhere.'

Judge Dee gave him a long look. The ugly man vaguely disturbed him. Why should Lo . . . ?

'You're wondering why Lo should've invited me, eh, Dee? The answer is that I am a poet. A writer of couplets, rather. My poems never contain more than two lines. You won't have read them, Dee. You're interested in official files!' He pointed with his thick forefinger at the dossier the judge was carrying.

'Let's go inside, sir, and have a cup of tea,' Judge Dee proposed, politely opening the door for him.

'No, thank you. I must fetch something from my room, then go out on an errand downtown.'

'Where are your quarters here in the compound, sir?'

'I stay in the fox shrine, right corner of the main courtyard.'

'Yes, Lo told me there was such a shrine here,' the judge said with a faint smile.

'Why shouldn't Magistrate Lo maintain a fox shrine, pray?' the sexton asked belligerently. 'Foxes are an integral part of universal life, Dee. Their world is as important or unimportant as ours. And just as there exist special affinities between two human beings, so some human beings are linked to a special animal. Don't forget that the signs of the zodiac that influence our destinies consist of animals, Judge!' He studied Judge Dee's face intently, rubbing his stubbly cheeks. Suddenly he asked, 'You were born in the year of the Tiger, weren't you?' When the judge nodded, the sexton's thick lips curved in a smirking grin that gave his ugly face a toad-like appearance. 'A tiger and a fox! Couldn't be better!' Abruptly his heavy features slackened; deep lines showed beside his fleshy nose. 'You'd better look sharp, Dee!' he said in a dull voice. 'There was one murder here last night, I hear, and things are shaping up for a second murder. That file under your arm is marked Yoo-lan, and she has a death sentence hanging over her head. Soon there'll be more dead walking with you, Dee!' He raised his large round head and again looked past the judge, a strange glint in his bulging eyes.

Judge Dee shivered involuntarily. He wanted to speak, but the sexton resumed, in his former querulous, rasping voice:

'Don't expect any help from me, Judge. I consider human justice a paltry makeshift, and I shan't lift a finger to catch a murderer! Murderers catch themselves. Run around in

53

circles even narrower than those of others. Never escape. See you tonight, Dee!'

He marched off, his straw sandals making a flapping sound on the court's pavement.

The judge looked after him, then quickly went inside, irritated at his own discomfiture.

The servants had drawn the curtains of the canopied bedstead in the rear of his room. He noticed with satisfaction the large padded tea-basket on the centre table, beside the tall pewter candlestick. Standing at the dressing-table, he rubbed his face and neck with the scented towel the servants had put ready in the brass basin. This made him feel better. Sexton Loo was just an eccentric, and such people liked to make extravagant statements. He pushed the table close to the open sliding-doors, and sat down facing his rock garden. Then he opened the dossier.

On top was Lo's biographical note on the poetess, about twenty folio sheets. It was an ably written account, so carefully phrased that the judge suspected that Lo planned to append it to his edition of Yoo-lan's poetical works. It stated all the relevant facts, sketching the background in veiled terms that could not give offence, but left no doubt about what was meant. After he had read the account carefully, the judge leaned back in his chair. Folding his arms, he went over in his mind Yoo-lan's checkered career.

The poetess was the only daughter of a small drug-shop clerk in the capital, a self-educated amateur of literature, who had taught her to read and write when she was only five years old. He was a bad financier, however. When she was fifteen, he had got so deeply in debt that he had to sell her to a famous brothel. During the four years she spent there, she assiduously cultivated old and young men of letters, and through these liaisons made rapid progress in all the elegant arts, showing a particular talent for poetry. At nineteen, when she was well on the way to becoming a fully-fledged, popular

54

courtesan, she suddenly disappeared. The guild of brothel-keepers sent out their best men to find her, for she represented a considerable investment, but they failed to trace her. Two years later she was discovered by accident in a low-class hostel up-country, destitute and ill. The man who found her was the young poet Wen Tung-yang, famous for his cutting wit, his good looks, and his vast inherited wealth. He had met her in the capital, and was still in love with her. He paid off all her debts, and she became his inseparable companion. No elegant gathering in the capital was deemed complete without the presence of Wen and Yoo-lan. Wen published a collection of poems they had written for each other, and these were cited in literary milieus all over the country. The pair travelled extensively, visiting all the famous scenic spots of the Empire, welcomed everywhere by famous men of letters, and often staying on for months in a place that caught their fancy. Their association lasted four years. Then Wen suddenly left her, having fallen in love with an itinerant female acrobat.

Yoo-lan left the capital for Szuchuan, where she used the generous parting present Wen had given her to purchase a beautiful country place. There she settled down with a bevy of maids and singing-girls, and her villa became the centre of intellectual and artistic life in that remote province. She granted her favours to carefully selected admirers only, all prominent men of letters and high officials who showered her with costly presents. Arrived at that point, Magistrate Lo hadn't been able to resist the temptation of quoting the hackneyed line, 'Each of her poems was valued at one thousand ounces of gold'. Lo also mentioned that Yoo-lan had a number of close girl friends, and some of her best poems were addressed to them. Read in connection with the fact that after a couple of years she had to leave Szuchuan abruptly because of complications caused by one of her students, the daughter of a local Prefect, the implication was obvious.

After having left Szuchuan, the poetess changed her way

of life completely. She bought the White Heron Monastery, a small Taoist shrine in the beautiful Lake District, and called herself a Taoist nun. She kept only one maidservant, no man was allowed inside, and she wrote only religious poetry. She had always spent her money as freely as she made it, and on leaving Szuchuan she had paid extravagant severance bonuses to all members of her numerous suite. The remainder she had invested in the purchase of the White Heron Monastery. But she was still considered well-to-do, for the notables living in that region paid her well for teaching poetry to their daughters. There Lo's biography ended. 'Please refer to the attached judicial documents,' he had written at the end of the page.

Judge Dee righted himself and quickly leafed through the bundle of legal documents. With his practised eye it took him little time to pick out the main facts. Two months before, in late spring, the constables of the local tribunal had suddenly entered the White Heron Monastery, and started digging under the cherry tree in the back garden. They found the naked body of Yoo-lan's maidservant, a girl of seventeen. The autopsy showed that she must have died only three days previously, from a cruel whipping that had lacerated her entire body. Yoo-lan was arrested, and accused of wilful murder. She scornfully denied the accusation. Three days previously, she said, the maid had asked for one week's leave to visit her aged parents, and she left after she had prepared the evening rice for her mistress. That was the last the poetess had seen of her. After she had taken her meal, she had gone out for a long walk along the edge of the lake, alone. When she came back one hour before midnight, she discovered that the garden gate had been forced, and upon checking found the two silver candlesticks in the monastery's chapel missing. She reminded the magistrate that the very next morning she had reported the theft to his tribunal. She suggested that the maid, having come back to the monastery because she had forgotten something, had surprised the robbers. They tried to make her tell

56

where her mistress's money was, and the maid succumbed under the torture.

Then the magistrate heard a number of witnesses, who testified that the poetess had often quarrelled violently with the maid, and that they had heard the maid scream sometimes at night. The monastery was located in an unfrequented neighbourhood, but a few pedlars had passed there on the fateful night, and they had not seen a trace of robbers or vagabonds. The magistrate declared Yoo-lan's defence a pack of lies, accusing her of having forced the garden gate herself and thrown the silver candlesticks into a well. Referring also to her lurid past, he was about to propose the death sentence, when armed robbers attacked a farmstead in the vicinity and cruelly hacked the farmer and his wife to pieces. The magistrate postponed judgement on Yoo-lan, and sent out his men to apprehend the robbers, who might prove Yoo-lan's story true. In the meantime the news of the arrest of the famous poetess had spread far and wide, and the Prefect ordered the case transferred to his own tribunal.

The Prefect's energetic investigation—he was an admirer of Yoo-lan's poetry—brought to light two points in her favour. First, it transpired that the magistrate had tried to obtain Yoo-lan's favours the year before, and that she had refused him. The magistrate admitted this but denied that the fact had influenced his dealing with the case. He had received an anonymous letter stating that a corpse was buried under the cherry tree, and he had deemed it his duty to verify that allegation. The Prefect ruled that the magistrate had been prejudiced, and temporarily suspended him from his duties. Second, the military police caught a robber who until a few weeks previously had been a member of the band that attacked the farmstead. He stated that their leader had talked about the poetess having a hoard of gold in the monastery, and added that it would be worth while having a look around there some time. This seemed to bear out Yoo-lan's theory about the murder. On the basis of these facts the Prefect passed the case on to the provincial tribunal, recommending acquittal of the accused.

The Governor, flooded with letters from high-placed persons all over the Empire in favour of the poetess, was about to give a verdict of not guilty, when a young water-carrier from the Lake District came forward. He had been absent for several weeks, accompanying an uncle on a journey to the family graves. He had been the maid's boy friend, and stated that she had often told him that her mistress importuned her, and beat her when she refused. The Governor's doubts were strengthened by the fact that the maid had been found to be a virgin. He reasoned that if robbers had murdered the maid, they would certainly have raped her first. He instructed the military police to search the entire province for the robbers who had attacked the farmstead, for their testimony was of course of vital importance. But all efforts to track the band down were in vain. Neither could the writer of the anonymous letter be traced. The Governor thought he had better wash his hands of this ticklish case, and referred it to the Metropolitan Court.

Judge Dee closed the dossier, arose from the table and went out on to the gallery. A cool autumn breeze rustled in the bamboos of the rockery, promising a fine evening.

Yes, his colleague had been right. It certainly was an interesting case. Disturbing, rather. He pensively tugged at his moustache. Magistrate Lo had described it as a purely theoretical puzzle. But his wily colleague had known very well, of course, that it would present him, the judge, with a personal challenge. And now his meeting with the poetess had linked him directly with her case, squarely confronting him with the question: guilty or not guilty?

The judge began to pace the gallery, his hands clasped behind his back. Secondary information was all he had on this disturbing, frustrating case. Suddenly the ugly, toad-like face

58

of the sexton rose before his mind's eye. That strange monk had reminded him that for the poetess this was a question of life or death. He was dimly conscious of a feeling of uneasiness, an inexplicable sense of foreboding. Perhaps he would rid himself of his vague discomfiture, if he tackled the dossier again and went over all the verbatim witness accounts. It was only five o'clock, so he still had two hours or so before the dinner would begin. Somehow or other, however, he didn't feel like resuming his study of the legal documents. He thought he would postpone that task till he had had a longer talk with the poetess, at dinner. Then he would listen also to what the Academician and the Court Poet had to say to her, try to gauge their attitude to the problem of her guilt. Suddenly the gay dinner party promised by his colleague took on the macabre significance of a court of justice, deliberating a death sentence. Now he had a distinct premonition of impending danger.

Trying to dispel these disquieting thoughts, he reviewed in his mind the murder of the student, Soong. That also was a frustrating case. He had taken part in the investigation of the scene of the crime, but now he could do nothing, had to depend entirely on what Lo's men would bring to light. There again he would have to work with second-hand information.

Suddenly the judge halted in his steps. His bushy eyebrows creased in a deep frown; he reflected for a while. He went inside, and took the booklet with Soong's musical score from the table. Apart from the student's historical notes, this was the only direct link with the dead man. Again he leafed through its closely written pages. Suddenly he smiled. It was a long shot, but it was worth trying! At any rate it would be better than sitting and moping here in his room, poring over statements by all kinds of persons he had never set eyes upon.

The judge quickly changed into a simple blue gown. Having put a small black skull-cap on his head, he went outside, the book under his arm.

VIII

Dusk was falling. In the front courtyard of the residence two maids were lighting the lampions hanging from the eaves of the surrounding buildings.

When he had joined the teeming crowd in the broad thoroughfare in front of the tribunal's main gate, Judge Dee heaved a deep sigh of contentment. His feeling of frustration had come mainly from his being cooped up in his colleague's palatial residence, isolated from the pulsating life of the city, a city practically unknown to him. Now that he was taking action, he felt better at once. He let himself be carried along by the throng, scanning all the while the gaudily decorated shop fronts. When he saw the shop-sign of a dealer in musical instruments, he elbowed his way towards the door.

He was met by a deafening din, for half a dozen customers were trying out drums, flutes and two-stringed fiddles, all at the same time. On the eve of the Mid-autumn Festival, every musical amateur was keen to prepare himself for the gay gatherings on the following day. The judge went to the office in the rear, where the owner was hurriedly gobbling down a bowl of noodles at his desk, one watchful eye on his assistants who were helping the customers. Visibly impressed by Judge Dee's scholarly air, the man got up at once and asked what he could do for him.

The judge handed him the musical score.

'All these are tunes for the straight flute,' he said. 'I wonder if you could identify them for me.'

After one glance at the notation the music dealer gave the book back to the judge, saying with an apologetic smile:

'We only know the simple score of ten signs, sir. This must be some ancient system of notation. For that you must consult an expert. Lao-liu is your man, sir. The finest flute-player in town, plays any tune at sight, in any notation, old or new. Lives close by, too.' He wiped his greasy chin. 'Only trouble is that Lao-liu drinks, sir. He starts at noon, after he has given his music lessons, and he is usually drunk by this time. He sobers up later in the evening, when he has to play at parties. Makes good money, but squanders it all on wine and women.'

Judge Dee put a handful of coppers on the table.

'Let one of your men take me to him, anyway.'

'Of course, sir. Thank you, sir! Hey there, Wang! Take this gentleman to Lao-liu's house. Come back here at once, mind you!'

As the young shop assistant was walking with Judge Dee down the street, he suddenly pulled his sleeve. Pointing at a wine shop opposite he said with a sly grin:

'If you want to do real business with Lao-liu, sir, you'd better buy him a little present. No matter how far gone he is, he'll wake up when you hold a jar of liquor under his nose!'

The judge bought a medium-sized jar of strong white liquor that was drunk cold. The youngster took him through a narrow passage to a dark, smelly back street, lined with ramshackle wooden houses, and lit only by the light that filtered through a dingy paper window here and there. 'The fourth house on your left sir!' Judge Dee gave him a tip and the boy scurried away.

The door of the flute-player's house was sagging on its hinges. From behind it came round curses, then a woman laughed shrilly. The judge put his hand against the panel and the door swung open.

In the small, bare room, lit by a smoking oil-lamp, hung an overpowering smell of cheap liquor. A fat man with a round, flushed face sat on the bamboo bench at the back. He wore baggy brown trousers, and a short jacket that was open in front, leaving his gleaming paunch bare. A girl was sitting on his knee. It was Small Phoenix. Lao-liu stared up at the judge with bleary eyes. The dancer quickly pulled her skirt down over her thighs, muscular and startlingly white, and fled to the farthest corner of the room, a fiery blush on her still, mask-like face.

'Who the hell are you?' the flute-player asked in a thick voice.

Ignoring the girl, Judge Dee sat down at the low bamboo table, and put the wine-jar down.

Lao-liu's bloodshot eyes grew wide.

'A jar of real Rose Dew, by heaven!' He came unsteadily to his feet. 'You're welcome, even if you look like the King of Hell himself, with that big beard! Open it up, my friend!'

The judge put his hand on top of the jar.

'You'll have to earn your drink, Lao-liu.' He threw the score book on the table. 'I want you to tell me what tunes are there.'

Standing at the table, the fat man opened the book with his thick but surprisingly nimble fingers. 'Easy!' he muttered. 'I'll freshen up a bit first, though.' He half-stumbled to the wash stand in the corner, and began to rub his face and breast with a soiled towel.

Judge Dee watched him in silence, still ignoring the dancer. What she was doing there was her own business. Small Phoenix hesitated, then she came up to the table and began timidly:

'I . . . I tried to persuade him to play at the dinner tonight, sir. He is a beast, but a marvellous musician. When he refused, I let him fondle me a bit . . .'

'I wouldn't play the blasted "Black Fox Lay" even if you lay with me till morning!' the fat man growled. He groped among the dozen or so bamboo flutes hanging from nails in the cracked plaster wall.

'I thought you were going to dance "A Phoenix among

A FLUTE-PLAYER QUARRELS WITH A DANCER

Purple Clouds",' the judge told her casually. He thought the dancer looked rather pitiful, with her still face and her bent narrow shoulders.

'Yes indeed, sir. But after . . . after I had seen the fine floor-space in the magistrate's hall . . . and after I had been introduced to those two high officials from the capital, and the famous Sexton Loo, I thought this was a chance that would never come again. Therefore I thought I might try to dance the other tune. It allows for a quick, whirling movement. . . .'

'Wriggle that small bottom of yours to decent music!' Lao-liu snapped. 'The "Fox Lay" is a bad tune.' He sat down on a low stool and opened the score book on his large knee. 'Hm, you don't want to hear the first, of course. "White Clouds Remind Me of her Dress, Flowers of her Face." Everybody knows that love song. The second looks like . . .' He brought the flute to his lips and played a few bars that had a fetching lilt. 'Oh yes, that's "Singing to the Autumn Moon". Quite popular in the capital last year.'

The fat man went through the score book, now and then playing a few bars to identify the tune. The judge hardly listened to his explanations. He was disappointed that his theory had come to nothing, but he had to admit it had been a far-fetched idea. The fact that the tunes had no titles and no words, and were written in a complicated notation he had never seen before, had suggested the possibility that it was no musical score at all, but the student's secret notes, written down in a kind of musical cipher. An obscene curse roused him from his thoughts.

'I'll be damned!' The flute-player was looking fixedly at the last tune in the book. He muttered, 'The first bars look different, though.' He put the flute to his lips.

Low notes came forth, in a slow, mournful rhythm. The dancer sat up with a startled look. The rhythm quickened; high, shrill notes formed a weird melody. The fat man lowered his flute. 'That's the blasted "Black Fox Lay"!' he said disgustedly.

The dancer bent over the table.

'Give me that score, sir! Please!' There was a feverish gleam now in her large, slanting eyes. 'With that score, any good flautist can play it for me!'

'As long as it isn't me!' the fat man growled, throwing the book on the table. 'I prefer to stay in good health!'

'I shall gladly lend you the book,' Judge Dee told the dancer. 'But you must tell me a bit more about that "Black Fox Lay". I am interested in music, you see.'

'It's a little-known, old local tune, sir, not included in any handbook for the flute. Saffron, the girl who acts as guardian of the Black Fox Shrine in the south city, is always singing it. I tried to make her write it down for me, but the poor thing is a half-wit; she can't read or write a thing, let alone a difficult musical score. Yet it's the most magnificent music to dance to. . . .'

Judge Dee gave her the book. 'You can return it to me tonight, at the dinner party.'

'Oh, thanks ever so much, sir! I have to rush off now, for the musician will want to practise it a bit.' In the doorway she turned round. 'Please don't tell the other guests that I am going to do this dance, sir. I want it to be a surprise!'

The judge nodded. 'Get two large bowls,' he told the fat man.

The musician took two earthenware bowls from the shelf while Judge Dee removed the stopper from the jar. He filled Lao-liu's bowl to the rim.

'High-class stuff!' the musician exclaimed, sniffing at the bowl. Then he emptied it in one long draught. The judge took a careful sip of his. 'Strange girl, that dancer,' he remarked casually.

'If she's a girl! Wouldn't wonder if she turned out to be a fox spirit, with a plumed tail under her skirt. Was just trying to find that out when you came in, sir!' He grinned, refilled his bowl and took a sip. Smacking his lips, he went on, 'Fox or not, she's great at squeezing the customers dry, the mercenary little bitch! Accepts their presents, lets them do a bit of kissing and patting, but as to real business, no, sir! No, never! And I have known her for over a year. Fine dancer she is, that I must say for her.' He shrugged his broad shoulders. 'Well, perhaps she's a wise one, after all. Come to think of it, I've seen many a good dancer go to pieces because of too much cavorting on the bed mat!'

'How did you come to know the "Fox Lay"?'

'Heard it many a year ago, from a couple of old crones. Midwives who made an extra penny by expelling evil spirits from the house of the expectant mother. Don't know the music too well, to tell you frankly. But the witch over there in the shrine, she's real good at it.'

'Who is she?'

'A blasted witch, that's what she is! A real fox spirit, that one! An old woman who picks rags found her in the street, nice little tot. That's what she seemed, at least! Grew up as a half-wit, didn't talk till she was fifteen. Then she got fits every so often, would roll her eyes and say strange, horrible things. The old crone got frightened, and sold her to a brothel. She was a looker, it seems. Well, the owner of the brothel pocketed a good fee from the elderly amateur who was going to deflower her. The old gentleman should've known better than to fool around with a fox girl. Let's have another one, sir, it's the first real drink I have had today.'

Having downed the bowl, the fat man sadly shook his head.

'The wench bit off the tip of his tongue when he tried to kiss her, then she jumped out of the window and ran off to the deserted shrine near the South Gate. And there she's been ever since. Not even the toughest bullies of the brothel guild dared to go there! Place is haunted, you see. Hundreds were slaughtered on that spot, man, woman and child. At night

66

you can hear their ghosts wailing on the piece of wasteland where the shrine stands. Superstitious people leave food at the tumbledown gate of the grounds, and the girl shares that with the wild foxes. Place is swarming with them. The girl dances around with them in the moonlight, singing that bl . . . blasted song.' His voice became slurred. 'That . . . that dancer is a fox too. Only one who dares to go there. Bl . . . blasted fox, that's what she is . . .'

Judge Dee got up. 'If you've to play tonight, you'd better go slow on that jar. Good-bye.'

He walked to the main street, and asked a pedlar how to get to the south city gate.

'It's quite a long way, sir. You've to walk down this street, then pass the big market, and go down the whole length of Temple Street. Go on straight from there, and you'll soon see the gate ahead.'

The judge hailed a small litter and told the two bearers to take him to the shrine at the southern end of Temple Street. He thought he had better get down there, and walk the rest of the way. For chairbearers are notorious gossips.

'You mean the Temple of Subtle Insight, sir?'

'Exactly. An extra tip if you make it quick.'

The men put the long shafts on their calloused shoulders and trotted off, with lusty heigh-hos to warn the crowd to make way.

IX

The judge pulled his robe closer, for in the open litter he felt the nip in the evening air. He was in high spirits, for the 'Fox Lay' might well prove to be the first real clue to the student's murder. The market was crowded with people and the stalls did a thriving business. But after they had turned into a broad, dark street, there were few people about. On either side rose high stone arches, alternating with long stretches of weatherbeaten brick walls. The judge learned from the inscriptions on the huge lanterns hanging from each gate that the main sects of the Buddhist creed were represented on Temple Street. The bearers lowered the litter in front of a two-storeyed gatehouse. The lantern suspended over the black-lacquered, double-door was inscribed with three large characters: 'Temple of Subtle Insight'.

Judge Dee stepped out. The two bearers began at once to rub their wet torsos dry. He told the elder one:

'You may take a rest here. I won't be longer than half an hour or so.' Handing him a tip, he asked, 'How long does it take to go from here to the east city gate?'

'If you go by litter, sir, it'll take you about half an hour. But if you know the short cuts by the crooked alleys, you'll get there much quicker on foot.'

The judge nodded. This meant that the murdered student could easily have visited the fox shrine near the South Gate. Entering the compound by the narrow door beside the main gate, he found the paved temple yard deserted. But there was light behind the window panes of the solid, two-storeyed main hall in the rear. To the right of the hall an open corridor ran along the outer wall of the compound. He walked along that corridor, for he planned to leave the temple by the back door and from there make his way to the south city gate. Thus the litter bearers would not know his real destination.

The corridor led to a narrow passage behind the main hall, between two dark, single-storey buildings which he took to be the quarters of the monks. The passage was dimly lit by a few small lanterns suspended from the eaves. He quickly walked on to the back gate at the end. While passing the window on the far corner of the building on his right he cast a casual look into the dark interior. Suddenly he stood stock still. He thought he had seen the sexton, sitting huddled up on the bench in the back of the bare room, and fixing him with his toad-like stare. The judge put his hands on the window sill and peered inside. He had been mistaken. In the faint light supplied by the lantern of the building opposite, he saw only a pile of monk's habits on the bench, with a skull-shaped wooden prayer-drum on top. He went on, angry with himself. Evidently he had been unable to rid himself of the disturbing image of the weird sexton.

He crossed the sparse pine forest behind the temple, keeping to the right. Soon he came out on a broad, well-paved highway. In the far distance the towering shape of the South Gate was outlined against the starry sky.

Glad that his manoeuvre had been successfully executed, he walked quickly down the street, lit here and there by the flickering oil-lamp on a pedlar's stall. On the left side were a few dark, abandoned houses, opposite him a mass of trees, growing from thick brushwood. There was a dilapidated stone gate. Just as he was about to cross, a long line of people came down the street. Their backs were bent under heavy packs and bags, but they were chattering merrily amongst themselves. Evidently they were leaving the city to spend the Mid-autumn Festival with their relatives up-country. Waiting to let the holiday-makers pass, the judge wondered where the Emerald Cliff would be, chosen by Magistrate Lo for the banquet the following night. Probably somewhere in the mountains to the west of the city. Studying the sky, he didn't see any drifting clouds near the bright autumn moon. However, the wood over on the opposite side of the road looked dark and forbidding. He went to the street-stall on his left and purchased a small storm lantern. Thus equipped he crossed the road.

Of the old gate only the two posts were left. Letting the light of his lantern shine into the greystone trough at the base of the left post, he saw there a pile of fresh fruit, and a rough earthenware bowl of cooked rice, half-covered with green leaves. These offerings proved that this was indeed the gate to the wasteland.

Judge Dee quickly parted the branches of the tangled undergrowth that barred the narrow pathway. After the first bend, he tucked the slips of his gown under the sash round his waist, and rolled up his long sleeves. Poking about in the brushwood he found a strong stick for pushing thorny branches out of the way, and continued along the winding path.

It was curiously still in this wilderness; he didn't even hear the cries of nightbirds. The only sound was the persistent drone of cicadas, and now and then a faint rustling in the thick undergrowth. 'The dancer is a plucky girl,' he muttered. 'Even in broad daylight this must be a dismal place!'

Suddenly he halted and tightened his grip on the stick. From the dark brush just ahead came a spitting sound. Two greenish eyes were glaring at him, about two feet above the ground. He quickly picked up a stone and threw it. The eyes disappeared. There was a commotion among the leaves, then everything was quiet again. So there were indeed foxes about. But they would never attack a man. Then, however, he was struck by a disturbing thought. He remembered having heard that rabies is of frequent occurrence among wild foxes and stray dogs. And a mad fox would attack anything in sight.

Pushing his skull-cap back, he reflected ruefully that he had perhaps acted a bit rashly by setting out on this trip unarmed. A sword or better still a short pike might have proved useful. But his leggings were thick, and the stick felt very serviceable, so he decided to go on anyway.

Soon the path broadened. Through the sparse trees he saw an extensive stretch of wasteland, bleak in the moonlight. A gentle slope, covered with tall grass and strewn with boulders overgrown with weeds, led up to the black bulk of a ruined temple. The outer wall had crumbled in several places, and the top-heavy curved roof of the single building inside was sagging badly. About half-way up the slope a dark shape jumped lithely on to a boulder, and sat down on its haunches. The judge saw clearly its pointed ears and long, plumed tail. The beast seemed unusually tall.

He peered for a while at the dark ruin, but could see no light or any other sign of life. With a sigh he went up the winding path marked by irregularly shaped stones. When he came near the fox, he raised his stick. The animal jumped down gracefully and streaked off into the darkness. The waving of the grass indicated that there were more foxes about there.

At the gate the judge halted to study the small front-yard, littered with rubbish. Mouldering beams were lying at the foot of the wall, and a faint stench of decay hung in the air. In the corner stood a life-size stone statue of a fox, sitting on its haunches on a high granite pedestal. The red rag draped round its neck was the only sign of human presence. The temple itself was a one-storey, square building of large bricks, blackened by age and overgrown with ivy. The right corner was crumbling away; it was there that the heavy roof was sagging dangerously. Here and there the tiles had dropped down, revealing the thick black roof beams. The judge went up the three granite steps and knocked with his stick on the lattice door. A section of the rotting woodwork fell down with a crash that sounded very loud in the still evening air. He waited, but no answer came from inside.

The judge pushed the lattice door open and stepped inside. A faint light came from the small side-hall on his left. He stepped round the corner, then stopped abruptly. Under a candle in a niche up in the wall, stood a tall, thin shape swathed in a soiled shroud. The head was a skull which stared at the judge with gaping, empty eyesockets.

'Let's save the mummery!' he said coldly.

'You ought to have screamed and run outside.' A soft voice spoke up directly behind him. 'Then you would have broken your legs.'

Slowly turning round, he found himself face to face with a young girl, very slim in a loose jacket of some rough, brown material, and long, torn trousers. She had a handsome but vacuous face with large, frightened eyes. But the point of a long knife was pressed against Judge Dee's flank, and her hand was quite steady.

'Now I have to kill you here,' she said in the same, soft voice.

'What a beautiful knife you have!' he said slowly. 'Look at that lovely blue sheen!'

As she lowered her eyes, he let his stick drop and quickly gripped her wrist. 'Don't be a fool, Saffron!' he snapped. 'Small Phoenix sent me. And I've seen Mr Soong.'

She nodded, biting her full lower lip. 'When my foxes got restless, I thought it was Soong,' she said, looking past him at the dummy. 'When I saw you coming up the path, I lit the light above my lover.'

The judge let go of her wrist. 'Can't we sit down somewhere, Saffron? I wanted to talk with you.'

'Only talk, not play,' she said earnestly. 'My lover is very jealous.' She slipped the knife into her sleeve and went up to the dummy. Straightening the patched shroud, she whispered, 'I won't let him play with me, dear! I promise!' She lightly

JUDGE DEE IN THE SHRINE OF THE BLACK FOX

tapped the side of the skull, then took the candle from the niche and passed through an arched door-opening in the wall opposite.

Judge Dee followed her into the small, musty-smelling room. She put the candle on the primitive table, made of rough boards, and sat down on a low bamboo seat. Except for a rattan stool there was no furniture, but in the corner lay a heap of rags which apparently served as her bed. The upper half of the back wall had crumbled away and the roof caved in so that part of the sky was visible. Thick clusters of ivy had crept through the gap and were hanging down along the rough bricks. Dry leaves came rustling down on to the dust-covered floor.

'It's very hot in here,' she muttered. She took off her jacket and threw it on the pile of rags in the corner. Her round shoulders and full breasts were smeared with dust. The judge tested the rickety rattan stool, then sat down. She looked past him with her vacant eyes, rubbing her bare breasts. Although he found the room quite chilly, he noticed that a thin rivulet of sweat came down in the hollow of her bosom, leaving a black streak across her flat belly. The mass of her tangled, untidy hair was bound up with a red rag.

'My lover looks very terrible, doesn't he?' she asked suddenly. 'But he has a good heart, never leaves me and always listens to me so patiently. The poor man had no head, so I chose the largest skull I could find. And every week I give him a new dress. I dig them up in the back-yard here, you know. There are many skulls and bones there, and nice pieces of cloth. Why didn't Soong come tonight?'

'He's very busy. He asked me to tell you that.'

She nodded slowly.

'I know. He's kept very busy sorting out all kinds of things. It happened so long ago—eighteen years, he says. But the man who killed his father is still here. When he has found him, he'll have his head chopped off. On the scaffold.'

74

'I am trying to find that man too, Saffron. What's his name again?'

'His name? Soong doesn't know. But he'll find him. If someone killed my father, I would also . . .'

'I thought you were a foundling?'

'I am not! My father comes to see me, sometimes. He's a nice man.' Suddenly she asked plaintively, 'Why then did he lie to me?'

Seeing the feverish gleam that had come into her eyes, the judge said soothingly:

'You must be mistaken. I am sure your father would never lie to you.'

'He did! He says he always keeps that scarf round his head because he is so ugly. But Small Phoenix met him after he left here the other night, and she says he isn't ugly at all. Why then doesn't he want me to see his face?'

'Where's your mother, Saffron?'

'She's dead.'

'I see. Who brought you up, then? Your father?'

'No, my old aunt. She was not nice, for she gave me to bad people. I fled, but they came after me here. First two of them, by day. I had gone up on the roof, carrying an armful of skulls and bones. When I dropped those on their heads, they ran away. Three of them came back, at night. But then my lover was there, and they screamed and rushed outside. One stumbled over a boulder, and broke his leg! You should've seen how the others dragged him off!'

She burst out laughing, a shrill sound that echoed in the bare room. Something rustled in the ivy. Judge Dee looked round. Four or five foxes had jumped from outside on to the top of the crumbling wall. They were fixing him with their strange, greenish eyes.

When he looked at the girl again, she had covered her face with her hands. A long shiver shook her thin body, but her shoulders were covered with sweat. The judge said quickly:

'Soong told me he often came here together with Mr Meng, the tea-merchant.'

She let her hands drop.

'A tea-merchant?' she asked. 'I never drink tea. Only the water from the well. And now I don't like that any more. . . . Oh yes, Soong told me he was living in the house of a tea-merchant.' She thought for a moment, then resumed with a slow smile, 'Soong comes every other night, bringing his flute along. My foxes like his music, and he likes me very much, said he would take me away to a nice place, where we could hear music every day. But he said I must tell no one, for he could never marry me. I told him I could never leave here and never marry anybody. For I have my lover, and I shall never part with him. Never!'

'Soong didn't tell me about your father.'

'Of course not! Father said I should never tell anybody about him. And now I've told you!' She shot him a frightened glance, then clasped her hand to her throat. 'I can hardly swallow . . . and I have such a terrible pain in my head, and in my neck. It becomes worse and worse. . . .' Her teeth began to chatter.

Judge Dee got up. The girl must be taken away from here the very next day. She was dangerously ill.

'I'll tell Small Phoenix that you aren't feeling well and we'll come to see you together, tomorrow. Has your father never asked you to come to stay with him?'

'Why should he? He said I couldn't be better off anywhere, looking after my lover and my foxes.'

'Better be careful with those foxes. When they bite you . . .'

'How dare you say that?' she interrupted angrily. 'My foxes never bite me! Some of them always sleep with me in the corner there, and lick my face. Go away, I don't like you any more!'

'I am very fond of animals, Saffron. But animals fall ill sometimes, just like us. And when they bite you, then you get sick too. I am coming back tomorrow. Good-bye.'

She followed him into the front-yard. Pointing at the statue of the fox, she asked timidly:

'I'd like to give that beautiful red scarf to my lover. Do you think the stone fox would be angry?'

The judge considered the problem. Deciding that for her safety the dummy had better stay as frightening as it was, he replied:

'I think the stone fox might get nasty about it. Better not take the scarf away from him.'

'Thank you. I'll make a mantle clasp for my lover, out of the silver hair-needles Soong promised me. Ask him to bring them tomorrow, will you?'

Judge Dee nodded and went through the old gate. Surveying the moonlit stretch of wasteland, he could not see a single fox.

X

Back in the pine forest behind the Temple of Subtle Insight, the judge left his lantern under a tree. When he had brushed himself down as well as he could, he entered the temple compound by the back gate. The window of the corner room where he thought he had seen the sexton was now shut.

Two monks stood talking together on the stairs of the main hall. He stepped up to them.

'I came to see Sexton Loo, but apparently he has gone out.'

'His reverence came here the day before yesterday, sir. But this morning he moved to the residence of His Excellency the Magistrate.'

The judge thanked them, and went to the main gate. His two litter bearers were squatting by the roadside, playing a gambling game with black and white pebbles. They quickly scrambled up. The judge told them to take him to the tribunal.

Upon his arrival at the residence, Judge Dee went straight into the main courtyard. He wanted to talk to Lo before the other guests arrived; after that he could change quickly into a more formal costume.

Half a dozen maids were rushing around in the elegant landscaped garden in front of the main hall, hanging coloured lampions among the flowering shrubs, and two boy servants were putting up a bamboo scaffolding for fireworks on the other side of the lotus pond. Looking up at the balcony of the second floor, the judge saw Magistrate Lo standing by the red-lacquered balustrade, talking with his counsellor. Lo wore an elegant wide robe of blue brocade, and a high winged cap of black gauze. Glad that the dinner had not yet begun, Judge Dee hastily ascended the broad staircase of polished wood.

When the small magistrate saw him coming along the balcony, he exclaimed, aghast:

'My dear fellow! Why haven't you changed yet? The guests'll be here any moment!'

'I have an urgent message for you, Lo. Personally.'

'Go and see whether the housemaster is managing all right in the banquet hall, Kao!' When his counsellor had gone inside, Lo asked rather curtly, 'Well, what is it?'

Leaning against the balustrade, Judge Dee told his colleague how the clue of the 'Black Fox Lay' had taken him to the deserted shrine, and the gist of his conversation there. When he had finished, the magistrate exclaimed, beaming at him:

'Magnificent, elder brother, magnificent! This means that we are half-way to the solution of our murder case, for we now know the motive! Soong came here to trace his father's murderer, but that chap got wind that the student was on his track, and he killed the poor fellow. It was Soong's notes concerning that old murder of eighteen years ago that the scoundrel searched for in the student's lodging. And found, too!' As Judge Dee nodded, Lo resumed, 'Soong consulted my archives for details of his father's case. We must now go over all dossiers of the Year of the Dog, and look for an unsolved murder, disappearance, kidnapping or what have you, involving a family of the surname Soong.'

'Any such case,' the judge corrected him. 'Since the student wanted his investigation to be a secret, Soong may be an assumed name. He planned to reveal his identity and file an official accusation as soon as he had found his man and collected proof of his crime. Well, the man murdered Soong, but now he has us on his heels!' Tugging at his moustache, he resumed, 'Another man I'd like to meet is Saffron's father. It's a shame that the heartless scoundrel lets his illegitimate child live in those filthy surroundings! And she's ill too. We must check with the dancer, Lo. She may have recognized Saffron's father, and if not she can give us at least a description of him,

79

for she saw him when he was leaving the ruin, with the scarf removed from his face. After we have located the fellow, we'll make him confess what woman he seduced, and see what we can do for the poor girl. Has Small Phoenix arrived yet?'

'Oh yes, she's in the improvised green-room, behind the banquet hall. Yoo-lan is with her, helping her with her make-up and so forth. Let's get her here. The other two dancers are also in the green-room, and we want to talk to the wench alone.' He looked over the balustrade. 'Holy heaven, the Academician and Chang are here! I must rush down to welcome them. You'd better hurry down the small staircase over there, Dee, and change as quickly as you can!'

Judge Dee went down the narrow staircase at the end of the balcony, and walked quickly to his own quarters.

While donning a dark blue robe with a subdued flower pattern, he reflected it was a pity that his imminent departure would prevent him from witnessing further developments in this intriguing murder case. After they had ascertained the identity of the student's father, murdered eighteen years ago, Lo would have to probe into the circumstances of his death, thoroughly investigating all persons who had had contact with him and who were still living in Chin-hwa. That would take many days, if not weeks. He, the judge, would personally see to it that Saffron was removed to suitable quarters. Then, after she had received medical attention, Lo should make her talk about her conversations with the murdered student. He wondered why the student had sought out Saffron. Only because of his interest in unusual music? That seemed most improbable. Soong did seem to have fallen in love with her, though. Meng's maid had mentioned Soong's preference for love songs, and the silver hair-needles he consulted the maid about now turned out to have been intended for Saffron. There were all kinds of interesting possibilities. He adjusted his winged velvet cap in front of the mirror on the dressing-table, then hurried back to the main courtyard.

He saw the shimmer of brocade robes on the brilliantly lit balcony. Apparently the guests were admiring the illuminated garden before dinner. This saved the judge from the embarrassment of entering the banquet hall when the high guests were already in their seats.

On the balcony, Judge Dee first made his bow to the Academician, resplendent in a flowing robe of gold brocade, and wearing the high square cap of the Academy, with two long black ribbons that hung down his broad back. Sexton Loo had put on a wine-red gown with broad black borders which lent him a certain dignity. The Court Poet had chosen a brown silk robe embroidered with a golden flower pattern, and a high cap with golden rims. Chang had indeed brightened up now; he was in animated conversation with Magistrate Lo.

'Don't you agree, Dee,' Lo asked briskly, 'that expressive force is one of the most striking features of our honoured friend's poetry?'

Chang Lan-po quickly shook his head.

'Let's not waste our precious time together on empty compliments, Lo. Ever since I asked to be relieved of my duties at Court, I have devoted most of my time to editing my poems of the past thirty years, and expressive force is exactly what my poetry lacks!' Lo wanted to protest, but the poet raised his hand. 'I shall tell you the reason. I've always led a placid, sheltered life. My wife is, as you may know, also a poet, and we have no children. We live in an attractive country house just outside the capital, I tending my goldfish and my tray-landscapes, my wife looking after our flower garden. Occasionally friends from the city drop in for a simple dinner, and we talk and write till far into the night. I always thought I was happy, until recently, when I suddenly came to realize that my poetry only mirrors an imaginary world, built up in my mind. Since my poems lack the direct link with real life, they have always been bloodless, devoid of life. And now, after my visit to my ancestral shrine, I keep asking myself

81

whether a few volumes of lifeless poems are sufficient justification for my fifty years' existence.'

'What you call your imaginary world, sir,' Lo said earnestly, 'is in fact more real than so-called real life. Our everyday, outer world is transitory; you grasp the permanent essentials of inner life.'

'Thanks for your kind words, Lo. Yet I feel that if once I could experience a shattering emotion, even a tragedy, something that entirely upset my placid existence, I would . . .'

'You're completely wrong, Chang!' the booming voice of the Academician interrupted. 'Come here, Sexton, I want your opinion too! Listen, Chang, I am getting on for sixty, am nearly ten years your senior. For forty years I have been a man of action, served in nearly every important branch of government, raised a large family, had all the shattering emotions a man can experience in public and private life! And let me tell you that only after my retirement last year, now that I am leisurely visiting all by myself the places I used to like, only now am I beginning to see through outer appearances, and to realize that the more permanent values lie outside our worldly life. You, on the contrary, could afford to skip that preliminary phase of action, Chang. You, my friend, have seen the Way of Heaven, without even looking out of your window!'

'So you quote Taoist texts!' the sexton remarked. 'The founder of Taoism was a garrulous old fool. He stated that silence is better than speech, then dictated a book of five thousand words!'

'I don't agree at all,' the Court Poet protested. 'The Buddha. . . .'

'The Buddha was a mangy beggar, and Confucius a meddling pedant,' the sexton snapped.

Judge Dee, shocked by the last statement, looked to the Academician for a fiery protest. But Shao just smiled and asked:

'If you despise all our three religions, Sexton, then where do you belong?'

'To nothingness,' the obese monk replied promptly.

'Oho! That's not true. You belong to calligraphy!' the Academician shouted. 'Tell you what we'll do, Lo! After dinner we'll have that enormous silk screen in your banquet hall down on the floor, and old Loo shall write one of his couplets on it. With a broom, or whatever he uses!'

'Excellent!' Lo exclaimed. 'The screen'll be treasured for generations to come!'

Now Judge Dee remembered having seen sometimes on the outer walls of temples and other monuments magnificent inscriptions in letters of more than six feet high, and signed 'Old Man Loo'. He looked at the ugly fat man with new respect.

'How do you manage to write those colossal inscriptions, sir?' he asked.

'I stand on a scaffolding wielding a brush five feet long. And when I inscribe screens, I do so while walking over a ladder laid across them. Better tell your servants to prepare a bucket of ink, Lo!'

'Who needs a bucket of ink?' the melodious voice of the poetess spoke up. Now that her face had been carefully made up, she was indeed a radiant beauty. And her olive-green gown was so cut as to disguise her somewhat portly figure. The judge watched the effortless ease with which she joined the general conversation, achieving just the right tone with the Academician and Chang: the familiarity of a colleague in letters, but with an undertone of deference. Only a long career as a courtesan could give a woman that ease in associating on equal terms with men not belonging to the family.

The old housemaster pushed the sliding-doors open, and Lo invited his guests to enter the banquet hall. Four thick, red-lacquered pillars supported the gaudily painted rafters, each pillar bearing an auspicious inscription in large golden characters. The one on the right read 'All the people enjoy together years of universal peace', the other giving the corresponding line, 'Fortunate in being ruled by a saintly and wise Sovereign'. The arched door-openings on either side had frames of intricately carved woodwork. The arch on the left gave access to a side-hall where the servants were warming the wine. In the side-hall opposite sat the orchestra of six musicians, two flautists, two violinists, one girl playing the mouth organ, and another sitting behind the large zither. While the orchestra struck up the gay melody 'Welcoming the High Guests', the small magistrate led the Academician and Chang ceremoniously to the seats of honour at the table directly in front of the enormous, three-panelled screen of white silk set against the back wall. Both protested that they were undeserving of that honour, but let themselves be persuaded by Lo. He invited Judge Dee to sit at the table on the left, so that he was Chang's neighbour, and then conducted the sexton to the upper place at the table on the right. After he had asked the poetess to be seated at Judge Dee's right hand, he himself sat down in the lowest place, next to Sexton Loo. Each table was covered by a piece of costly red brocade, with gold-embroidered borders; the plates and bowls were of choice coloured porcelain, the wine cups of pure gold, and chopsticks of silver. The platters were heaped with seasoned meat and fish, slices of pressed ham, preserved ducks' eggs, and countless other cold delicacies. And although the hall was lit by the high floor lamps along the walls, there stood on each of the three tables two tall red candles in holders of wrought silver. After the maids had served the wine, Magistrate Lo raised his cup and drank to the health and good fortune of all present. Then they took up their chopsticks.

The Academician at once began to exchange news with Chang about mutual acquaintances in the capital. Thus the judge was free to address the poetess. He inquired politely

84

when she had arrived in Chin-hwa. It turned out that she had arrived two days before with the armed escort, consisting of a sergeant and two soldiers, and had taken a room in a small inn behind the Sapphire Bower. She added, without a trace of embarrassment, that the old lady in charge had worked in the same famous brothel in the capital she herself had belonged to, and that she had looked her up to talk about the old days. 'I met Small Phoenix in the Sapphire Bower,' she added. 'A superb dancer, and a very bright girl.'

'She seemed a bit over-ambitious to me,' Judge Dee remarked.

'You men never understand women,' the poetess said dryly. 'Which is probably very fortunate—for us!' She cast an annoyed look at the Academician who had set out on an elaborate speech.

'Thus I am certain I speak for all of you when I tender our profound thanks to Magistrate Lo, gifted poet, excellent administrator, and a perfect host! We thank him for gathering here, on the eve of the auspicious Moon Festival, this small group of old friends, congenial spirits, united in perfect harmony at this festive dish!' Turning his flashing eyes to the poetess, he said, 'Yoo-lan, you'll compose for us an ode in praise of the occasion! The theme is "The Happy Reunion".'

The poetess took up her wine cup and turned it round in her hand for a few moments. Then she recited in her rich, ringing voice:

> The amber wine is warm in the golden cups,
> Roast and venison are fragrant
> In the silver dishes
> And the red candles burn high.

As she paused, Magistrate Lo nodded with a pleased smile. But the judge noticed that the sexton was watching the poetess with an uneasy glint in his bulging eyes. Then she recited the parallel couplet:

THE BANQUET IN THE RESIDENCE

But the wine is the sweat and blood of the poor,
Roast and venison their flesh and bones,
And the red candles
Drip with their tears of despair.

There was a shocked silence. The Court Poet had grown
red in the face. Giving the poetess an angry look, he said,
mastering his voice with difficulty:

'You refer to conditions that obtain only temporarily, Yoo-
lan. And in regions struck by floods or droughts.'

'They obtain always and everywhere. And you know it!'
she told him curtly.

Magistrate Lo quickly clapped his hands. The musicians
began a gay, fetching melody, and two dancing-girls came
drifting in. Both were very young. One wore a long, flowing
dress of transparent white gauze, the other an azure-blue robe.
After they had dropped a low curtsey in front of the main
table, they lifted their arms above their heads and began to
turn slowly, the ends of their long sleeves whirling around
them in wide circles. While the one danced on the tips of her
tiny feet, the other bent one knee, and they alternated these
postures in quick succession. It was the well-known number
'Two Swallows in Spring', and although the girls did their
best, they seemed conscious of their nakedness under the thin
robes, and lacked the abandon of experienced dancers. The
guests did not pay much attention to them and there was a
general conversation while the servants brought in steaming
hot dishes.

Judge Dee covertly observed the drawn face of his neighbour who was listlessly picking at her food. He knew from
her biography that she had actually experienced abject
poverty, and he appreciated her sincerity. But her poem had
been unkind to their genial host, rude, even. He bent over to
her and asked:

'Don't you think your poem was a bit unkind? I know that

despite his debonair manner Magistrate Lo is a most conscientious official, who uses his private means not only for entertaining us, but also for contributing generously to all charitable organizations.'

'Who wants charity?' she asked with disdain.

'Wanted or not, it still helps a lot of people,' Judge Dee remarked dryly. He couldn't make out this strange woman.

The music stopped and the two young dancers made their bow. There was half-hearted applause. New dishes were being carried to the tables, and fresh wine was brought out. Then Lo rose from his chair, and said with a broad smile:

'The performance you witnessed just now was but a modest introduction to the main programme! After the stewed carp has been served, there'll be a brief interval, for watching the fireworks in the garden, from the balcony. Afterwards you'll see a rare old dance, peculiar to this region. It'll be performed by the dancer Small Phoenix, accompanied by two flutes and the small drum. The title of the melody is "Black Fox Lay".'

He resumed his seat amidst the astonished murmur of the guests.

'Excellent idea, Lo,' the Academician shouted. 'At long last a dance I've never seen before!'

'Very interesting,' the Court Poet commented. 'As a native of this district, I know that there exists an old fox-lore here. Never heard about that particular dance, though.'

The sexton asked Lo in his hoarse, croaking voice:

'Do you think it's right to have a magic dance at this . . .'

The rest was lost in the animated music the orchestra had struck up. Judge Dee wanted to start another conversation with the poetess, but she said curtly:

'Later, please! I like this music. Used to dance to it, formerly.'

The judge devoted his attention to the carp stewed in a sweet-sour sauce which was indeed delicious. Suddenly a swishing sound came from outside. A rocket flew up, leaving a string of coloured lights in its wake.

'On to the balcony, please!' Magistrate Lo shouted. And to the housemaster who was standing by the screen, 'Douse all the lights!'

They all rose and went out on the balcony. Judge Dee stood himself at the red-lacquered balustrade, beside the poetess. Lo was on her other side, and Counsellor Kao and the old housemaster stood a little further along. Looking over his shoulder, the judge vaguely saw the tall figure of the Academician. He supposed that Chang and the sexton were standing there too, but he couldn't see them for all the lamps and candles had been put out and the banquet hall was a mass of indistinct black shadow.

A large wheel consisting of coloured lights was turning round on the scaffolding in the garden below, sparks spouting from the fire crackers attached to its circumference. It turned quicker and quicker, then suddenly dissolved in a rain of multicoloured stars.

'Very pretty!' the Academician remarked behind Judge Dee.

There followed a bouquet of flowers that after a while exploded loudly into a flight of butterflies. Then came a long series of symbolical figures, in dazzling colours. The judge wanted to begin a conversation with the poetess, but he thought better of it when he saw her wan, drawn face. Suddenly she turned to Lo and said:

'You are doing us very well, magistrate. It's a magnificent spectacle!'

The self-deprecatory remarks of her neighbour were drowned in a series of loud detonations. Judge Dee inhaled with satisfaction the acrid powder smell that rose up from the garden. It cleared his head a little, for he had drunk many cups, and in quick succession. Now there appeared a large tableau, representing the conventional triad of the characters for Happiness, Riches and Long Life. There was a last burst of crackers, then the garden grew dark.

'Thanks very much, Lo,' the Court Poet said. He had come up to the balustrade, together with the Academician and Sexton Loo. While they were complimenting the magistrate, Yoo-lan said in a low voice to the judge:

'That conventional triad is very silly. If you're happy, riches'll make you unhappy, and a long life'll make you outlive your happiness. Let's go inside, it's getting chilly here, and they are lighting the candles again.'

When the guests were resuming their places, six servants came in carrying steaming dishes of dumplings. The poetess had not sat down.

'I'll go and see whether Small Phoenix is ready for her dance,' she told the judge. 'The girl hopes to establish a reputation by performing before this select company, you know. Dreams of getting invited to the capital, I bet!' She went to the arched door-opening behind their table.

'I propose a toast to our generous host!' the Academician called out.

They all raised their wine cups. The judge picked up a dumpling. It was stuffed with chopped pork and onions, flavoured with ginger. He noticed that the sexton had been served a special vegetarian dish of fried bean-curd; but he did not touch it. He was crumbling a piece of candied fruit in his thick fingers, his protruding eyes fixed on the door-opening through which the poetess had disappeared. All of a sudden Magistrate Lo let his chopsticks clatter down on the table. With a smothered exclamation he pointed at the door. Judge Dee turned round in his chair.

The poetess was standing in the archway. Her face deadly pale, she was looking dazedly at her hands. They were covered in blood.

XI

As she began to sway on her feet, the judge, who was nearest to her, jumped up and took her arm. 'Are you wounded?' he asked sharply.

The poetess looked up at him with vacant eyes.

'She . . . she's dead,' she faltered. 'In the green-room. A gaping wound . . . in her throat. I . . . I got it on my hands. . . .'

'What the devil does she say?' the Academician shouted. 'Did she cut her hands?'

'No, it seems that the dancer had an accident,' Judge Dee told them soberly. 'We'll see what we can do for her.' He beckoned to Lo, and led the poetess outside; she leaned heavily on his arm. In the side-hall Counsellor Kao and the house-master were giving instructions to a maid. They gave the poetess a startled look, and the maid let the tray she was carrying clatter down on to the floor. As Magistrate Lo came rushing outside, the judge told him in a whisper, 'The dancer was murdered.'

Lo snapped at his counsellor:

'Run to the main gate and tell them to let no one pass! Order a clerk to call the coroner!' And to the housemaster: 'See to it that all the gates of the residence are locked at once, then call the matron!' Swinging round to the dumbfounded maid, he barked, 'Take Miss Yoo-lan to the anteroom at the end of the balcony, make her comfortable in an armchair and stay with her till the matron arrives!'

Judge Dee had pulled the napkin from the maid's sash and now he quickly wiped Yoo-lan's hands. There was no wound. 'How do we get to the green-room?' he asked his colleague, handing the fainting woman over to the maid.

'Come along!' Lo said briskly and went down a narrow side-passage along the left side of the banquet hall. He pushed open the door at the end, then halted with a gasp. After a quick glance at the dark flight of stairs that led down opposite the door, Judge Dee followed him inside the narrow, oblong room that smelled of sweat and perfume. No one was about there, but the light of the high, white-silk floor lamp shone on the half-naked body of Small Phoenix, lying on her back across the ebony bench. She was clad only in a transparent underrobe; her white, muscular legs hung down on to the floor. Her thin bare arms were flung out, her broken eyes stared up at the ceiling. The left side of her throat was a mass of blood that was slowly spreading on the reed-matting of the bench. Fingermarks in blood stood out on her bony shoulders. Her heavily made-up, mask-like face, with its long nose and distorted mouth that showed a row of small sharp teeth, reminded the judge of the snout of a fox.

Magistrate Lo put his hand under one of her small, pointed breasts.

'Must've happened only a few minutes ago!' he muttered as he righted himself. 'And there's the murder weapon!' He pointed at a pair of scissors on the floor, stained with blood.

While Lo bent over the scissors, Judge Dee cast a quick glance at the woman's garments, neatly folded on the chair in front of the simple dressing-table. On the high clothes-rack in the corner hung a voluminous green silk robe with wide sleeves, a red sash and two long scarves of transparent silk. Turning to his colleague, he said:

'She was killed as she was about to slip into that dancing-robe.' He picked up the student's score book from the table, and put it in his sleeve. His eyes fell on a small door, at a right-angle to the one through which they had come in. 'Where does this lead to?'

'To the banquet hall. It's right behind the wall screen.'

Judge Dee turned the knob. When he had opened the door

a crack, he heard the voice of the Court Poet: '. . . that Lo keeps a physician on the premises. For . . .'

Pulling the door shut softly, the judge said:

'You'll want to have a good look around, Lo. Don't you think I'd better go back to the banquet hall, and deputize as host?'

'Please do, Dee! Glad you said it was an accident. Let's keep to that; it won't do to upset the guests. Say she cut herself with a pair of scissors. See you later, when I have questioned everybody.'

The judge nodded and went out. He told the cluster of frightened servants in the side-hall to go about their business, and re-entered the banquet hall. Resuming his seat, he said:

'The dancer let her scissors drop on her right foot, and a vein was cut. The poetess tried to staunch the blood, but she got faint and rushed back to us for help. I'll deputize for Lo, if I may.'

'Trust a woman to lose her head on such an occasion!' the Academician said. 'Glad it wasn't Yoo-lan who hurt herself. I am sorry for that Phoenix girl, though. But I can't say I mind missing that fox dance. We are gathered here for a more exalted purpose than to watch a wench tripping about!'

'Hard luck for a dancer to hurt her foot,' the poet remarked. 'Well, now that we are four, we might as well forego all formality. Why don't we have these three tables turned into one? If Yoo-lan picks up again, we'll make room for her.'

'Very good!' the judge exclaimed. He clapped his hands and ordered the servants to push the two side-tables up against the main one. He and the sexton moved their seats up, so that now they sat facing Shao and Chang across the improvised square table. He motioned the maids to refill their cups. After they had drunk to the speedy recovery of the dancer, two servants brought a tray with roasted duck, and the orchestra began another melody. The Academician raised his hand and shouted:

'Tell'm to take that tray back, Dee! And send those fiddlers away too. We've had plenty to eat, and plenty of music! Now we can start to drink in earnest!'

The Court Poet proposed another toast, then Sexton Loo, and Judge Dee toasted the three guests on behalf of their absent host. The Academician involved the poet in a complicated discussion of the merits of classical prose as compared with modern styles. This permitted the judge to engage Sexton Loo in conversation. The sexton had been drinking heavily; his vows evidently didn't include abstinence from wine. The film of moisture covering his coarse face made him resemble a toad more than ever. Judge Dee began:

'Before dinner you said you were not a Buddhist, sir. Why then do you retain the title of sexton?'

'The rank was bestowed upon me when I was young, and it stuck,' the other replied gruffly. 'Undeservedly, I admit. For I leave it to the dead to bury their own.' He emptied his cup in one draught.

'There seem to be many Buddhists in this district. I noticed a street lined by half a dozen Buddhist temples. Had only time to look at one, the Temple of Subtle Insight. What denomination does it belong to?'

The sexton looked him over with his bulging eyes which now had a curious reddish gleam.

'To none. They have found that the shortest way to the ultimate truth lies in one's own self. We don't need the Buddha to tell us where and how to discover it. There are no gaudy altars, no holy books, no noisy religious services. It's a quiet place and I always stay there when I come here.'

'Hey, Sexton!' the Academician called out. 'Chang here tells me that his own poems are getting shorter all the time! He'll end up by writing some of two lines only, just like you!'

'I wish I could!' the poet said wistfully. His cheeks were flushed. The judge thought Chang couldn't stand his drinks as well as the Academician, whose heavy-jowled, pale face was as impassive as ever. Shaking his head, the poet went on, 'At first sight your lines seem trite, Sexton; sometimes they don't even seem to make sense! Yet you can't put them out of your mind, and one day you suddenly see the point. A special toast to our great couplet poet, gentlemen!'

After they had emptied their cups, the poet resumed:

'Now that we have the place to ourselves, so to speak, why don't you inscribe that screen for our host, eh, Sexton? Your unrivalled calligraphy'll compensate Lo for all the good toasts he is missing!'

The ugly monk set down his wine cup.

'I'll dispense with your levity, Chang,' he said coldly. 'I take my work seriously.'

'Ho ho, Sexton!' the Academician shouted. 'We'll have none of your excuses. You don't dare to write, because you've had too much. I bet your legs are getting wobbly already! Come on, it's now or never!'

The Court Poet burst out laughing. Ignoring him, the sexton told the judge quietly:

'It'll be quite a job to get that big screen down, and the servants are all in a dither. If you get me a sheet of paper, I'll write a poem for our host here at the table.'

'All right!' the Academician told him. 'We are magnanimous! Since you are too drunk to write your enormous characters, we'll let you off with one tiny little inscription. Tell those chaps to bring ink and paper, Dee!'

Two servants cleared the table, and a maid brought a roll of blank paper and a tray with writing implements. Judge Dee selected a sheet of thick white paper of five by two feet and smoothed it out on the table while the sexton rubbed the ink, mumbling something with his thick lips. When the fat monk took up the writing-brush, the judge put his hands on the upper end of the paper to keep it steady.

The sexton rose. He stared for one brief moment at the paper, then his hand shot out and he wrote two lines, each in

96

practically one sweep of the brush, as quickly and surely as the lash of a whip.

'By heaven!' the Academician exclaimed. 'This is indeed what the ancients called inspired writing! Can't say I care much for the content, but the calligraphy is worthy of being engraved into stone, for posterity!'

The Court Poet read the lines aloud:

'"We all return to where we came from: Where the flame went of the doused candle." Care to explain the meaning, Sexton?'

'I don't.' The sexton selected a smaller brush, and dedicated the poem to Magistrate Lo, signing it in one flourish: 'Old Man Loo'.

Judge Dee told the maids to stick the sheet up on the central panel of the wall screen. It struck him that it was an apt epitaph for the young dancer whose dead body was lying in the room behind.

Counsellor Kao came in. Bending over, he whispered something in Judge Dee's ear. The judge nodded and said:

'My colleague told me to inform you, gentlemen, that to his profound regret he has to forego the honour of attending upon you. The poetess Yoo-lan asks to be excused also, for she has a splitting headache. I hope that the distinguished company will kindly consent to make do with me as deputy host.'

The Academician emptied his cup. Wiping his moustache, he said:

'You are doing very well, Dee, but I think we'll call it a day, eh, gentlemen?' He got up. 'We'll thank Lo tomorrow morning, when we view the Moon altar together.' Judge Dee conducted him to the broad staircase, the counsellor following them with the poet and the sexton. Going down, Shao said with a broad smile:

'Next time the two of us must have a longer talk, Dee! Eager to hear your views on administrative problems. I am always interested in hearing what younger officials have to say about . . .' Suddenly he gave the judge a doubtful look, as if debating whether he hadn't already said all this. He solved the problem by concluding jovially, 'Anyway, I'll see you tomorrow! Good night!'

After Judge Dee and Counsellor Kao had seen the three guests off and taken leave of them with many low bows, the judge asked:

'Where's the magistrate, Mr Kao?'

'In the anteroom down here in the main hall, sir. I'll lead the way.'

The small magistrate was sitting at the tea-table, hunched up in an armchair, his elbows on the table, head bent. Hearing the judge come inside, he looked up with haggard eyes. His round face was drawn; even his moustache was drooping.

'I am lost, Dee,' he said hoarsely. 'Ruined completely. For good!'

XII

Judge Dee pulled up another chair and sat down opposite his colleague.

'It can hardly be as bad as all that,' he said soothingly. 'It's never pleasant to have a murder in your own residence, of course, but such things happen. As to the motive of this brazen murder, it'll interest you that the flute-player downtown, whom I consulted about Soong's musical score, told me that Small Phoenix was an expert in fleecing her customers. A girl who encourages men, then refuses them at the last moment, is liable to make bitter enemies. I suppose one of those utilized the bustle of caterers and tradesmen going in and out of here for slipping inside unnoticed, and reached the green-room by that dark flight of stairs I noticed opposite the door.'

Lo had hardly listened. Now, however, he lifted his head and said wearily:

'The door at the bottom of that staircase has been locked as long as I've lived here. My womenfolk aren't always as obedient as one would wish, but I am still far removed from putting the Consort's Staircase to use.'

'A consort's staircase? What on earth is that?'

'Ah, well, you don't read modern poetry, do you? Fact is that the notorious Ninth Prince who resided here twenty years ago was not only a traitor, but a henpecked husband to boot. Some say it was the goading and nagging of his consort that made him attempt his ill-fated rebellion. It was she who ruled "from behind the screen", as the saying goes. She had that room behind the banquet hall built, and the flight of stairs, which connects down below with a corridor leading straight to the women's quarters. There was a high screen standing in the rear of the hall, then as now. When the prince was sitting on his throne in front of the screen, holding an audience, his consort went to that room and stood herself behind the screen, listening to the proceedings. If she knocked on the screen once, the prince knew he had to say no, if twice he could say yes. The story became so well known that the term "consort's staircase" is now widely used as a literary allusion, meaning a henpecked husband.'

Judge Dee nodded. 'Well, if the murderer couldn't get to the green-room by the backstairs, how then did he manage to . . .'

Lo heaved a deep sigh, sadly shaking his head.

'Don't you see it, Dee? It was that confounded poetess who did it, of course!'

The judge sat up in his chair. 'Impossible, Lo! Do you mean to say that Yoo-lan went into the green-room just when the dancer . . .' He broke off in mid-sentence. 'Holy heaven!' he muttered. 'Yes, she could've done just that, of course. But why, in the name of heaven?'

'You read the biographical account I wrote, didn't you? I made things sufficiently clear there, I trust. She had got fed up with men. When she met Small Phoenix, she took a fancy to her. I thought it was a bit strange that she personally took the dancer to my office. "My dear this" and "my dear that"! Tonight she came to the banquet hall well ahead of time, to help the dancer prepare for her dance. Prepare, my foot! She hung about in that green-room for more than half an hour! Tried to make up to the wench, of course. The dancer threatened to lodge a complaint. During the first half of the dinner that blasted poetess worked out a plan to silence her.'

'Just because the dancer threatened to complain?' the judge asked, incredulous. 'Yoo-lan couldn't care less! In the past she has had a number of . . .' He clapped his hand to his forehead. 'My humble apologies, Lo! I am very dense to-night! Merciful heaven, an official complaint by the dancer could've brought Yoo-lan to the scaffold! It would support the testimony of the murdered maid's lover, and turn the scales against her!'

'Exactly. The affair that forced her to leave Szuchuan was effectively hushed up. The girl concerned being a Prefect's daughter, there was no danger of any damaging evidence coming from that quarter. But imagine a professional dancer appearing in court, delivering a frank testimony, with all the lurid details, about an offence committed right here, next door to the hall where an official banquet was being held! It would settle Yoo-lan's hash, once and for all! The poetess was desperate.' He rubbed his podgy hand over his moist face. 'But not more desperate than I am now! It was my good right, as magistrate of this district, to detain an accused being escorted across my territory. But I had to give the sergeant in charge of her guarantee, of course. Stating in black and white, and over my seal and signature, that I am completely responsible for the prisoner as long as she is under my roof. And now the woman has committed a murder here, and a murder of exactly the same nature as the one she stands accused of! The damned cheek of it! She expects me to gloss over the crime, of course, report it as committed by the famous unknown intruder from outside. So as to save her skin and mine! But there she's got me wrong!'

The magistrate sighed and went on sombrely:

'It's damned hard luck, Dee! As soon as I have reported this disgraceful affair, the Metropolitan Court will suspend me, as guilty of dereliction of duty and criminal negligence. I'll be condemned to hard labour on the frontier—if I am lucky, that is! To think that one of my reasons for inviting the woman here was to earn the praise of the panjandrums in the capital, for a kind gesture made to a famous poetess in distress!' He pulled a large silk handkerchief from his sleeve and mopped his face.

Judge Dee leaned back in his chair. He knitted his bushy

eyebrows. His friend was in a very nasty predicament indeed. The Academician could pull strings for him, of course, try to have the case dealt with in the capital behind closed doors. Publicity wouldn't be good for the Academician's town reputation either. On the other hand . . . no, he was going much too fast. Taking hold of himself, he asked quietly:

'What did the poetess say?'

'She? When she comes into the green-room, she says, and sees the dancer lying there bleeding like a pig, she rushes up to her, and tries to raise her by her shoulders, to see what's wrong! When she sees she's dead, she rushes to us for help. At this moment she's languishing on a couch in my First Lady's room, being pampered with cold towels and what have you!'

'Didn't she say anything about who could have done it?'

'Oh yes. Came across with the same information that flute-player downtown gave you, only with a different slant. Yoo-lan maintains that Small Phoenix was a pure girl, and many nasty, nasty men hated her for that! Says a rejected suitor slipped inside and killed her. Thus suggesting to me the easy way out! I left her without making any comment, only asked her to keep to the story of the dancer's accident, for the time being.'

'What about the coroner's report?'

'Nothing there we didn't know or couldn't have guessed, Dee. Confirmed she had been killed shortly before we saw her, ten, fifteen minutes at the most. Added that she was a virgin. Which doesn't astonish me a bit. That pinched face, flat bosom! Well, the last people who saw her alive were two young dancing-girls, who brought Small Phoenix tea and cakes just before they packed up and went back to the Sapphire Bower. Then the wench was as right as rain.'

'What did the servants say? And the musicians?'

'Still thinking of that unknown intruder, eh? No such luck! Have been questioning everybody, together with my counsellor. The musicians watched the fireworks from the side-hall, and none of them left the room. And all that time there were a number of servants about, on the main stairs, and on the staircases at either end of the balcony. Impossible for your unknown intruder to have got up to the second floor unnoticed. Grilled everybody about a possible connection with the dancer. Nothing doing. She was a pure girl, remember! Also, that pair of scissors was of course a typical woman's weapon. Fine, complete case! Beautifully simple.' He pounded the table with his fist. 'Great heavens, what a trial it'll be! Nation-wide sensation! And me on the wrong side of the bench, mind you! A disgraceful ending to a promising career!'

The judge remained silent for some time, pensively caressing his sidewhiskers. At last he shook his head doubtfully.

'There is an alternative solution, Lo. But I am afraid you won't like that either!'

'Can't say you are a comforting kind of chap, elder brother. But let's have it anyway. A man in my desperate position'll clutch at a straw!'

Judge Dee put his elbows on the table.

'There are no less than three other suspects, Lo. Namely your three distinguished dinner guests.'

The small magistrate jumped up.

'You've had one too many, Dee, at dinner!'

'I probably had. Else I'd have thought earlier of the alternative. Go back to when we were watching the fireworks from the balcony, Lo. Can you visualize us as we were standing there at the balustrade? The poetess was on my left, and you were standing beside her. A little further on were your counsellor and your housemaster. Now although your firework display was lovely, I did look about me from time to time, and I know that none of us stirred from the balustrade. But I don't know about Shao, Chang and the sexton, who were somewhere behind us. I got a glimpse of the Academician once at the beginning, and again at the very end of the display, when he came forward together with Chang and Sexton Loo. Did you see any one of them while the fireworks were going on?'

The magistrate, who had been pacing the floor, now halted and resumed his seat.

'When the fireworks started, Dee, the Court Poet was standing close behind me. I offered him my place, but he said he could see very well over my shoulder. And I got a glimpse of Sexton Loo, who was standing beside Chang. In the middle of the display I wanted to apologize to the sexton for the lack of Buddhist motifs among the symbolical figures, but when I looked round I saw nobody—the banquet hall was pitch dark, and my eyes were blinded by the flares of the fireworks.'

'Just as I feared. Well, you yourself pointed out to me just now that every poet knows the story of the Consort's Staircase, complete with the room behind the hall, and the door in the wall concealed by the screen. That means that each of your three guests had a splendid opportunity to murder the dancer in the green-room. They knew in advance she was there, because you had announced she would dance directly after the fireworks. Plenty of time to work out a simple and effective plan. When the servants had put out all the lights, and everybody was watching the garden, the murderer stepped back into the hall, slipped behind the screen and into the green-room. While saying a few kind words, he picked up the pair of scissors and killed her. Then he came coolly back to the balcony by the same route. Can't have taken him more than three minutes, all of it.'

'What if he had found the door locked, Dee?'

'In that case he could have afforded to knock, for your fireworks were making a great deal of noise. And if he had found a maid together with Small Phoenix, he could just say that the fireworks bored him, and that he had dropped in for a friendly chat. Postponing his murderous plan for a subsequent occasion. It was a perfect set-up for murder, Lo.'

'It certainly was, if you come to think of it,' Lo said pensively, pulling at his short moustache. 'But good heavens, Dee, isn't it absurd that one of these great men would . . .'

'How well do you know them, Lo?'

'Well . . . you know how it is with those famous persons, Dee. I've met all three of them a couple of times, but always in company, and we talked about literature, and art, and so on. No, I know very little about their real characters. But look here, elder brother! Their careers are public property! If any of them had a strange streak in him, people would have . . . Except as regards the sexton, of course. He'd stick at nothing, absolutely nothing! Fellow wasn't always as unworldly as now, you know. Formerly he administered a large tract of ecclesiastical property in the Lake District, and used to bleed the tenant farmers white. Later he repented, of course, but . . .' He smiled wanly. 'To tell you the truth, I haven't yet digested this new development, Dee!'

'I quite understand, Lo. It is indeed a bit of a shock when you have to consider those three illustrious persons as murder suspects. As to the sexton, he wrote a beautiful scroll for you, at the dinner table. I had it stuck up on the wall screen. Well, let's forget all about great talent and exalted position, and consider our three men just as ordinary suspects in a murder case. We know all three had the opportunity. The next question is that of motive. The first thing is to make inquiries about the dancer in the Sapphire Bower. All of your three guests seem to have been in Chin-hwa for a day or two already, which means that they may have met Small Phoenix before she was introduced to them this afternoon. How did she meet them, by the way?'

'Oh, when I was going upstairs with Shao and Chang to show them the banquet room, Yoo-lan and the dancer were just coming down, and I introduced her. Afterwards I saw from the balcony that Small Phoenix ran into Sexton Loo, in front of my fox shrine. He's staying in the small room behind the shrine, you know.'

'I see. Well, when you're back from the Sapphire Bower, we must try to find in the archives which dossier Soong had been studying there. For . . .'

'Holy heaven! The murdered student! Two murders to solve! Wait, what did my housemaster tell me again about Soong's landlord? Oh yes, his chaps nosed about in that quarter, but the tea-merchant is a popular man there. Not a breath of scandal or shady dealings. I think his eagerness to foist his theory of the vagrant ruffian on us was just an attempt to show off his cleverness. Most people love to act the amateur detective, you know!'

'Yes, we may count Meng out. I had been toying with the idea that Soong might have had a secret love-affair with Meng's daughter. She's a good-looking young girl, and her maid told me she could hear in her room the sentimental tunes Soong played on his flute at night. If Meng had learned about the liaison . . . However, now we know that it was Saffron Soong was fond of, and that he wanted to buy the silver trinkets for her. And Soong mentioned his landlord to Saffron, without saying a word about suspecting him of having murdered his father, so we have absolutely nothing against the tea-merchant.' He smoothed his long black beard. 'To come back to Small Phoenix. We were going to ask her for a description of Saffron's father. You might inquire in the Sapphire Bower whether the dancer ever mentioned there that the guardian of the Black Fox Shrine was an illegitimate child, and that her father was still about here in Chin-hwa. Let's draw up a programme for tomorrow, Lo. First, your visit to the Sapphire Bower. Second, a search in your old archives, for the eighteen-year-old case that interested the murdered student. Third . . .'

'You'll have to take care of the Sapphire Bower for me, Dee! I promised my wife and children that I would take my guests to view the Moon Altar they built in the fourth court-yard, and I am supposed to do that tomorrow morning. If my old mother feels well enough, she'll be there too.'

'All right, I'll visit the Sapphire Bower directly after break-fast. Please send a letter of introduction over to my quarters, Lo, for the lady in charge there. Then I'll join all of you to see the Moon Altar, and as soon as possible afterwards the two of us can go to the chancery and consult the archives together. As to my third point, I'll have to see to that alone. Namely, go to the Black Fox Shrine, and persuade Saffron to leave that horrible place. You have a secluded corner here where she can stay, I suppose?' When his colleague nodded, the judge went on slowly, 'It won't be easy to wean her away from her foxes and that ghastly lover of hers, but I hope I'll be able to handle her. Talking about Saffron, Lo, I must tell you that Sexton Loo was staying in a temple very near the wasteland. And he has a weird theory that some human beings have a special affinity with foxes.' He tugged at his moustache. 'It's a pity I didn't ask Saffron whether her father was thin or heavy.'

'Nonsense, Dee!' Lo said impatiently. 'Saffron told you that, according to the dancer, the man was good-looking!'

Judge Dee nodded approvingly. Despite his absent-minded airs, his colleague was a very good listener.

'She did indeed, Lo. But Small Phoenix may have said that just to please the poor girl. I shall go after luncheon to the ruined temple to get her so that I have the whole afternoon for that delicate job. Unless, of course, the Prefect should summon me.'

'Heaven forbid!' Magistrate Lo shouted, aghast. 'Can't tell you how grateful I am, Dee! You have given me a ray of hope!'

'A very thin ray only, unfortunately. What time were you thinking of starting the banquet on the Emerald Cliff, by the way? The place lies outside the city, I suppose?'

'It does. Our most famous scenic spot, elder brother! High up on the nearest mountain range, about half an hour by litter from the west city gate. At the Mid-autumn Festival one's supposed to ascend a high place, as you know! There's a pavilion there, on the edge of a century-old pine forest. You'll love it, Dee! The servants'll go ahead in the afternoon, to prepare everything. We'll have to leave here about six, so that we'll be there in time to admire the sunset.' He got up. 'It's past midnight, and I am dog-tired, Dee. I think we'd better be off to bed. I'll just nip upstairs for a moment, though, to have a look at the scroll Sexton Loo wrote for me.'

Judge Dee had risen too.

'You'll find the writing magnificent,' he said. 'But the contents suggest that he knew the dancer was dead.'

XIII

Judge Dee woke up early. He pushed open the sliding-doors and went to stand on the verandah in his nightrobe, to enjoy the fresh morning air. The rock garden was in shadow; a thin film of dew still covered the bamboo leaves.

No sound came from the residence behind him. Everybody seemed to be late. It must have taken the servants till long after midnight to tidy up after the banquet. From the tribunal compound in front, however, there came shouted commands, and the clatter of arms. The guards were going through the morning drill.

After a leisurely toilet the judge dressed in a wide robe of blue silk and put a square cap of stiff black gauze on his head. He clapped his hands and told the heavy-eyed boy servant to bring him a tea-basket and a bowl of rice gruel with pickles. The boy came back carrying a tray heaped with food: steaming white rice, assorted pickled vegetables, cold chicken, crab omelette, stewed bean curd, a bamboo box with fritter cakes, and a dish of sliced fresh fruit. Apparently such a luxurious breakfast was the rule in the residence. Judge Dee told him to move the table outside, under the eaves of the verandah.

Just after he had started breakfast, a clerk brought him a sealed envelope. It was a note from his colleague:

Elder Brother,

The housemaster is taking the dancer's body to the Sapphire Bower. He shall impress on them that it is in their own interest to keep the case secret till tomorrow, when I shall deal with it in the tribunal. Please find enclosed a letter of introduction addressed to the lady in charge.

Your ignorant younger brother, Lo Kwan-choong.

The judge put the letter in his sleeve and told the clerk to take him to the side entrance of the tribunal, explaining that he wanted to take a morning stroll. On the corner of the street he rented a small litter, and ordered the bearers to take him to the Sapphire Bower. Being carried through the streets, crowded with early market-goers, he wondered how his colleague had managed to keep the fact that the dancer was dead from his host of servants. Probably the wily old housemaster had made the necessary arrangements. The bearers lowered the chair in front of a simple black-lacquered door in a quiet, residential street. The judge was just about to tell them that it must be the wrong address, when he noticed the two letters 'Sapphire Bower' inscribed on a discreet small brass plaque on the doorpost.

When the surly gatekeeper had admitted him he found himself in a well-kept paved courtyard, decorated by a few flowering plants in basins of sculpted white marble. Over the red-lacquered double-gate at the rear was a white board, inscribed in large blue letters 'Among the Flowers reigns Eternal Spring'. It was not signed, but the calligraphy resembled closely that of his colleague.

A broad-shouldered rascal with a pockmarked face accepted Judge Dee's letter with a dubious expression, but when he saw the large red stamp of the tribunal on the back, he made an obsequious bow. He led the judge along an open corridor lined by red-lacquered, carved balustrades, round a charming flower garden, to a small anteroom. Judge Dee sat down at the tea-table of polished sandalwood. The blue pile carpet was soft under his feet, and blue brocade hangings covered the walls. Smoke of ambergris curled up from the white-porcelain incense burner on the wall-table of carved rosewood. Through the open sliding-doors he could just see a corner of the two-storeyed building facing the garden. From the gilded lattice-screens along the balcony came the tinkling of zithers. Apparently the inmates were already at their music lessons.

A large woman in a black damask gown came in, followed by a demure maid carrying a tea-tray. Folding her hands in her long sleeves, the madame delivered a polite speech of welcome. The judge took in her pasty face with the pendulous cheeks and the crafty, beady eyes, and decided he didn't like her. 'Has the housemaster of the residence already arrived?' He cut her harangue short.

She told the maid to put the tea-tray on the table and to leave them alone. Straightening her robe with her large, white hand, she said:

'This person profoundly regrets the unfortunate accident, sir. I do hope it did not inconvenience the honourable guests.'

'My colleague informed them the dancer only wounded her foot. Could you get me her papers?'

'I knew you would want those, sir,' she replied with a smirk.

She took a bundle of documents from her sleeve and handed them to the judge. He saw at once that there was nothing of special interest. Small Phoenix had been the youngest daughter of a vegetable dealer, sold three years ago for the simple reason that she had four elder sisters already, and her father couldn't afford any more dowries. The house had her taught to dance by a well-known teacher, and she had also received tuition in elementary reading and writing.

'Did she have any special friends among the customers, or among the inmates here?' the judge asked.

The madame ceremoniously poured him a cup of tea.

'As to the gentlemen who patronize this establishment,' she said quietly, 'nearly all of them knew Small Phoenix. Being a superb dancer, she was in great demand for parties. Since she wasn't exactly handsome, only a few elderly gentlemen solicited her special favours, doubtless attracted by her boyish figure. She always refused, and I refrained from exercising pressure on her, for she brought in enough by her

111

dancing.' A slight frown appeared on her smooth white brow as she continued, 'She was a quiet girl, never needed any correction, and was most diligent about her dancing lessons. But the other girls hated her, they said she . . . smelled, and that she was really a vixen that had assumed human shape. It's an onerous task, sir, to preserve order among all those young women. . . . Asks for much patience, and kind consideration of . . .'

'She didn't engage in a bit of blackmail now and then?'

The madame raised her hands in protest.

'I beg your pardon, sir!' she exclaimed, giving him a reproachful look. 'All my girls know that the first who would dare to try anything irregular would find herself standing stripped at the whipping post, at once! This house has an old-established reputation, sir! Of course she accepted tips, and . . . well, it seems she was rather skilful in raising the amount, by ah . . . various but wholly acceptable means. Since she was an obedient girl, I allowed her to visit sometimes the strange woman who acts as guardian of the Black Fox Shrine. Only because she taught Small Phoenix interesting songs that proved popular with the guests.' She compressed her thin lips. 'All kinds of vagabonds hang about in the neighbourhood of the South Gate, sir. She must have struck up an undesirable acquaintance there, and it was he who perpetrated this cruel crime. Goes to show one should never let those girls out of sight. If I think of the good money I invested in her dancing lessons, and . . .'

'Talking about the guardian of the fox shrine, was it from this house she escaped, formerly?'

For the second time the madame gave him a reproachful look.

'Certainly not, sir! That girl had been sold to a small place near the East Gate. A very low-class house, frequented by coolies and other scum. A . . . a brothel, sir, with your permission.'

'I see. Did Small Phoenix ever mention that the guardian of the shrine was not an orphan, and that her father was still living in this city?'

'Never, sir. I once asked the dancer whether the woman ever received gentlemen . . . callers, but she said she was the only one who ever visited the shrine.'

'The poetess Yoo-lan was greatly distressed about the dancer's demise. Was there any special interest, on either side?'

The madame lowered her eyes.

'The honourable Yoo-lan was visibly impressed by the dancer's shy, youthful deportment,' she replied primly. Then added quickly, 'And by her great talents, of course. I am most tolerant of female friendships, sir. And since I had the honour to know the poetess in the capital, formerly . . .' She shrugged her heavy shoulders.

Judge Dee got up. While the madame was conducting him to the gate, he remarked casually:

'His Excellency the Academician, the Honourable Chang Lan-po and His Reverence Loo were all disappointed not to see Small Phoenix dance. They must have seen her perform before, I imagine.'

'That seems hardly possible, sir! Those two illustrious persons honour this district with a visit sometimes, but they never partake in any public or private parties. It's the talk of the town that they have accepted His Excellency's invitation this time! But His Excellency Lo is such a wonderful man! Always so kind and understanding. . . . What was the name of the religious gentleman you mentioned, sir?'

'It doesn't matter. Good-bye.'

Back in the tribunal, Judge Dee had a clerk announce him to Magistrate Lo. He found his colleague in his private office, standing in front of the window, his hands clasped behind his back. He turned round and said listlessly:

'Hope you slept well, Dee. As for me, I had a rotten night! One hour after midnight I crept into the main bedroom, thought that was my best bet for a good night's rest, for my First Lady always goes to sleep early. But I found her wide awake, with my Third and Fourth standing in front of her bed, shouting at each other! My First said I had to resolve their quarrel. In the end I had to accompany my Fourth, and she kept me awake for another hour, telling me in great detail how the quarrel had begun!' Pointing at the large official envelope on his desk, he added dramatically, 'That letter was brought for you by a special messenger from the Prefecture. If it's a summons from the Prefect, I'll jump into the river!'

Judge Dee slit the letter open. It was a short official notice that, the Prefect not requiring his presence, the judge should return to his post without undue delay. 'No, I am ordered back to Poo-yang. I'll have to leave here tomorrow morning, at the latest!'

'Heaven preserve me! Well, that leaves us today, at least. What did you find out from the madame?'

'Only facts that aggravate the case against Yoo-lan, Lo. First, the poetess did indeed conceive a liking for the dancer. Second, none of our three guests has ever visited the Sapphire Bower and the madame thought it most unlikely any of them had ever met the dancer before.' As the small magistrate nodded morosely, he asked, 'Do you know what our guests' plans are for this afternoon?'

'At four we'll gather in the library, to read and discuss together my latest volume of verse. And to think I had been looking forward to that session so eagerly!' He sadly shook his round head.

'Do you think that your housemaster's men are good enough at their job to follow one of your guests, should he go out after the noon rice?'

'Good heavens, Dee! To follow them, you mean?' Then he shrugged resignedly. 'Well, my career is probably ruined anyway. Yes, I think I could take the risk.'

'All right. I also want you to order the sergeant in charge

of the South Gate to post two armed guards in one of the street-stalls opposite the entrance to the wasteland, to keep an eye on the gate. Let them arrest anyone who wants to visit the Black Fox Shrine. I wouldn't want anything untoward to happen to that poor girl there, and I might need the men when I go there myself, this afternoon. Where are your guests now?'

'They're having breakfast. Yoo-lan's with my First Lady. That gives me time to take you to the chancery archives, Dee!'

He clapped his hands, and when the headman appeared, he ordered him to proceed personally to the South Gate and instruct the sergeant of the guard. On his way out he was to tell Counsellor Kao that he was wanted in the archives.

The magistrate took Judge Dee through a maze of corridors to a cool, spacious room. The walls were covered up to the lofty, coffered ceiling with broad shelves, loaded with red leather document boxes, ledgers and dossiers. There was an agreeable smell of wax, used for polishing the boxes, and of the camphor strewn among the papers to keep insects away. At one end of the huge trestle table in the centre of the red-tiled floor, an old clerk was sorting out some papers. At the farthest end Sexton Loo sat bent over a file.

XIV

The obese sexton was now dressed in a brown robe of hemp, fastened on his left shoulder by a clasp of rusty iron. He gravely accepted the greetings of the two magistrates, then listened silently to Lo's effusive thanks for the scroll he had written for him the night before. Then he tapped the dossier in front of him with his thick forefinger and said in his hoarse voice:

'Dropped in here to read up on the peasant revolt, two hundred years ago. There was a massacre at the South Gate. If all the people who were then put to the sword were still about there, you wouldn't be able to shoulder your way through the gate! You need this particular file, Lo?'

'No, sir. Just came to locate a document.'

The sexton gave him his toad-like stare.

'You did, did you? Well, if you can't find it, just seal this room, and light a stick of incense in your fox shrine. When you come back here, you'll find the dossier you want sticking out beyond the others on those shelves. The fox spirit'll help an official. Sometimes.' He shut the file and got up. 'Well, isn't it time to view your Moon Altar?'

'I'll take you there now, sir! Hope you'll join us later, Dee. Ha, there's my counsellor! Help my colleague to find his way among the dossiers, Kao!'

Lo went out, respectfully opening the door for the sexton.

'What can I do for you, sir?' Mr Kao asked in his precise voice.

'I was told that in the Year of the Dog there occurred an unsolved murder here, Mr Kao. I'd like to have a look at the dossier on that case.'

'The Year of the Dog is notorious because of the conspiracy

116

of the Ninth Prince, sir! But an unsolved murder, no, I don't remember ever having read about that. Perhaps the greybeard over there'll know, sir. He was born and bred here! Hey there, Liu, do you recall an unsolved murder in the Year of the Dog?'

The old clerk thought, fingering his ragged chinbeard.

'No, sir. It was a bad year for us here in Chin-hwa, all right, with the high treason of General Mo Te-ling. But no unsolved murder, no, sir.'

'I have read about the case of General Mo,' Judge Dee remarked. 'He was a confederate of the rebellious Ninth Prince, wasn't he?'

'Oh yes, sir. All the documents are in that large red box, up on the fifth shelf on the right there. The paperbound dossiers beside it deal with other judicial cases of that same year.'

'Let's get the whole lot down here on the table, Mr Kao.'

The old clerk put the stepladder up against the shelves, and took the files down one by one, handing them to the counsellor who placed them in chronological order on the table. As the row grew longer and longer, Judge Dee realized the magnitude of his task. It needn't have been an unsolved murder, of course. It might as well have been a case recorded as solved, but where an innocent man had been convicted. His accuser was then technically the murderer of the executed man.

'You keep the archives in excellent order, Mr Kao,' he remarked. 'There isn't a speck of dust on them!'

'I have the clerks take all the dossiers down once every month, sir,' the counsellor said with a pleased smile. 'The boxes are polished, and the documents aired, which also keeps insects out!'

The judge reflected that in this case it was a pity that the archives were in such a spick-and-span condition. If these old files from the upper shelves had been covered with dust, recent smudges might tell which ones the student had been consulting.

'The murdered student used to work here at this table, I suppose?'

'Yes, sir. The files stacked on the lower shelf there are those regarding the peasant revolt which Soong was studying. A very intelligent young man, sir, with a wide interest in administrative problems. When I came in here, I often found him also reading files of a more recent date. A serious research worker, never tried to keep me here for a talk. Well, this is the lot, sir.'

'Thank you. I won't keep you from your work, Mr Kao. If I need a particular document, I shall ask the old clerk.'

When the counsellor had taken his leave, Judge Dee sat down at the table and opened the first dossier. The greybeard returned to the papers he was sorting out at the other end of the table. Soon the judge was immersed in a variety of criminal cases. One or two posed interesting problems, but none suggested a miscarriage of justice, and the name Soong occurred only once, as defendant in a minor case of fraud. When a young clerk brought fresh tea, he learned to his astonishment that it was already one hour before noon. The clerk informed him also that the magistrate was still in the fourth courtyard of the residence, together with his guests. It seemed that the noon meal would be served there too.

Heaving a sigh, the judge decided he would tackle the box containing the papers relating to General Mo Te-ling's high treason. A man found guilty of a crime against the State was executed together with all his accomplices, and it was not impossible that one of those had been falsely accused.

As soon as he had opened the box, a thin smile of satisfaction curved his lips. The folders the box was packed with had been stuffed carelessly inside and not in the correct sequence. In these exceptionally well-kept archives, this was a sign he was on the right track. The student had evidently consulted this file, and hastily put the folders back when someone entered the room. He carefully arranged the dossiers on the table according to their serial numbers.

The first one gave a summary of the case against the Ninth Prince. It was suggested in guarded terms that the prince had been of unbalanced mind: morbidly suspicious, subject to fits of deep depression, jealous and quarrelsome. After he had nearly killed a courtier in a fit of rage, the Emperor had relegated him to the palace in Chin-hwa, hoping that the quiet life there would have a beneficial influence. However, the prince had begun to brood over imagined wrongs. His toadying courtiers kept assuring him that he was the favourite prince of the nation, and his ambitious, masterful consort goading him, he finally conceived the fantastic plan of fomenting a rebellion and usurping the Dragon Throne. When he tried to win for his cause some disgruntled civil and military officials, the clumsy plot leaked out. The Emperor despatched a Censor with full executive powers to Chin-hwa, accompanied by a regiment of Imperial Guardsmen. The guards surrounded the palace, and the Censor summoned the prince and his consort for questioning. He told the prince that the Emperor knew everything, but was willing to forgive him, on condition that he ordered his bodyguard to surrender their arms, and that he and his consort would return to the capital at once. The prince drew his sword and killed his consort on the spot, then cut his own throat. The guards entered the palace and placed the inmates under arrest while the Censor confiscated all documents. This happened on the fourth day of the second month, eighteen years ago.

That same day the Censor opened the investigation. All courtiers who had been cognisant of the scheme and all other accomplices of the prince were summarily executed. For although the Emperor had been willing to forgive the prince because of his sick mind, there was no excuse for the other plotters. During the hectic days that followed a number of false accusations were filed—evil people trying to utilize the

119

opportunity for ridding themselves of personal enemies, as often happens in such serious cases with wide ramifications. The Censor had sifted these accusations, most of them anonymous, with meticulous care. Among them was a long, unsigned letter, stating that the retired General Mo Te-ling had been in the plot, and that incriminating correspondence with the Ninth Prince could be found hidden in such and such a place, in the general's women's quarters. The Censor had the general's mansion searched, the letters were indeed found in the place indicated, and he was arrested on a charge of high treason. The general denied everything, maintaining that the letters were forged and planted in his mansion by some old enemy. Now the Censor knew that General Mo, thinking he had been passed over for promotion, had resigned from the service before his time and gone into retirement in his native district of Chin-hwa, brooding over his wrongs. Former associates of the general testified that he had often talked to them about impending changes, that would give all able men a chance to come into their own. The Censor studied the letters and found them perfectly authentic. The general was convicted and executed together with his two adult sons, as dictated by the harsh law on high treason. All his possessions were confiscated by the State.

Judge Dee leaned back into his chair. It was a fascinating account, and the fact that he was studying it here in the same tribunal where the sensational trial had been enacted gave it an immediacy that most old legal documents lacked. The judge selected the file listing the members of the general's household and his confiscated possessions. Suddenly he sucked in his breath. The general had had three wives, and two concubines. The surname of the second concubine was Soong. There were no further details about her, for she had not been questioned: she had committed suicide by hanging herself on the evening of the third day of the second month, one day before the Censor had arrived in Chin-hwa. She had given the general one son, named I-wen, who had been five years old when disaster struck the Mo household. Everything fitted! This was, at long last, the clue he had been hoping to find! He sat back in his chair with a satisfied smile.

Suddenly, however, the smile froze on his face. The student had come back to avenge his father. This could only mean that Soong had discovered proof that General Mo had been innocent, that he suspected the writer of the anonymous letter of having planted the evidence, and therefore considered him as his father's murderer. And the fact that this unknown man had murdered the student was irrefutable proof that the student had been right. Heavens, there had been a terrible miscarriage of justice, eighteen years ago!

The judge took the dossier with the record of the hearing of the case. Slowly tugging at his whiskers, he read it through. There was but one point in General Mo's favour, namely that none of the other plotters had known that the Ninth Prince had won the general to his cause. The Censor, however, had dismissed this on the grounds that the Ninth Prince had been over-suspicious, and distrusted his own confederates. He had based his case on the letters found in the general's residence. These were in the handwriting of the prince, on his own private letter-paper, and provided with his own personal seal.

Shaking his head, Judge Dee selected the text of the anonymous letter. It was a chancery copy in the indifferent handwriting of a clerk, all original documentary evidence having been forwarded to the capital. But judging by the impeccable style, it must have been written by an accomplished man of letters. In the margin was a copy of the Censor's personal comment: 'This letter probably emanates from a disgruntled courtier. Check content and handwriting at once.' Reading the next document, Judge Dee found that despite all efforts by the Censor's men the writer had not been identified. The government had issued a proclamation promising him a substantial reward, but no one had come forward to claim it.

Slowly stroking his long beard, the judge considered the case. It would have been impossible to forge the letters from the Ninth Prince, authenticated with the personal seal he always wore on his person. Also, the Censor had enjoyed the reputation of absolute integrity, a most capable criminal investigator, who had brilliantly solved a number of other difficult cases involving highly placed persons. Judge Dee remembered that his own father, the late State Counsellor, had sometimes talked about those cases, highly praising the Censor's acumen. Since he had found the general guilty, he must have been completely sure of his case. The judge got up and began to pace the floor.

What new evidence could the student have obtained? He had been only five years old when it all happened, so it had to be either hearsay or documentary evidence. How to trace what Soong had discovered? The student had been murdered, and the murderer had abstracted the documents Soong had concealed in his lodging. The family of Soong's mother seemed the first possibility that had to be explored. He beckoned the old clerk and asked:

'Are there many families of the surname Soong here?'

The greybeard nodded ponderously.

'A great many, sir. Rich and poor, related and unrelated. In olden times this county was called Soong, you see.'

'Get me the Register of Taxes of the Year of the Dog, the section Assessment, but only the part dealing with families of the surname Soong.'

When the old man had placed an open ledger on the table, the judge consulted the section of the lowest-income Soongs. Since Soong's mother had been only a second concubine, her father must have been a tenant farmer, small shopkeeper or artisan. There were only half a dozen items. The third regarded Soong Wen-ta, owner of a vegetable shop, one wife and two daughters; the eldest married to a hardware dealer named Hwang, the younger one sold to General Mo as second

JUDGE DEE CONSULTS THE ARCHIVES

concubine. Judge Dee put his forefinger on the item and said:

'Please find out in this year's Population Register whether Mr Soong is still alive.'

The old clerk went to the shelves on the side wall and came shuffling back with an armful of thick rolls. He unrolled a few and peered at the closely written entries, mumbling in his beard, 'Soong Wen-ta . . . Soong Wen-ta . . .' At last he looked up and shook his head. 'He and his wife must have died without male issue, sir, for no one of that particular Soong family is listed any more. Do you wish to know in what year they died, sir?'

'No, that's not necessary. Give me the list of members of the Guild of Hardware Dealers!' The judge got up from his chair. This was the last chance.

The greybeard opened a large box marked 'Minor Guilds'. He selected a thin booklet and handed it to the judge. While the old man gathered up again the rolls of the Population Register, Judge Dee leafed through the booklet. Yes, there was a hardware dealer called Hwang, married to a woman of the surname Soong. The item was marked by a small circle in the margin, meaning that Hwang was in arrears with the payment of his membership fees. He was living in an alley near the East Gate. Judge Dee memorized the address, then he threw the booklet on the table with a satisfied smile.

Bending over the dossier of the Mo household, he verified that after the execution of the general the family had scattered. The dead concubine's son, Soong I-wen, had been adopted by a distant uncle in the capital. The judge detached from the file the copy of the anonymous letter accusing the general and put it into his sleeve. He thanked the old clerk, and told him he could replace all the files. Then he walked over to the residence.

On approaching the fourth courtyard, the judge was greeted by the shouts and laughter of children. It was a charming scene. About two dozen children, all dressed up in gaudy costumes, were romping about the man-high Moon Altar, which had been erected in the centre of the paved yard. On top of it was the white figure of the long-eared Moon Rabbit, fashioned out of dough and standing on a pile of Moon Cakes —round flour-cakes stuffed with sweet beans. At the base was a profusion of platters and bowls heaped with fresh fruit and sweetmeats, and at the corners high red candles and bronze incense burners; these would be lit after dark.

Judge Dee crossed the yard to the broad marble terrace where a small group of people stood watching: the Court Poet and Sexton Loo at the marble balustrade, Lo, the Academician and the poetess behind them, beside a capacious armchair of carved ebony, set on a low dais. In the armchair sat a frail old lady in a long black dress, her snow-white hair combed back straight from her forehead. She held in her wrinkled hands an ebony walking-stick with a handle of green jade. Behind the chair stood a tall, handsome woman of middle age, very stiff and erect in a close-fitting robe of embroidered green silk. She was evidently Magistrate Lo's First Wife. The two dozen or so women hovering in the shadows of the hall behind her would be his secondary wives with their personal maids.

Ignoring all others, the judge stepped up to the Old Lady and made a low bow in front of the dais. While she was surveying him with her keen old eyes, Lo bent over to her and whispered respectfully:

'This is my colleague Dee from Poo-yang, Mother.'

The old lady nodded her small head, and bade the judge welcome in a soft but surprisingly clear voice. He inquired respectfully after her age, and learned she was seventy-two.

'I have seventeen grandchildren, Magistrate!' she announced proudly.

'A virtuous house is blessed by numerous progeny, Milady!' the Academician pronounced in his loud voice. The old lady bobbed her head with a pleased smile. Judge Dee greeted Shao, then paid his respects to the Court Poet and

Sexton Loo. Finally he inquired after the health of the poetess. She replied that she was feeling all right, thanks to the good care of the magistrate's First Lady. But the judge thought her face looked drawn and wan. He took his colleague apart and told him in a low voice:

'The student was a son of General Mo Te-ling, by an unofficial concubine of the surname Soong. He came here to prove that his father had been falsely accused. Exactly as he told Saffron. He didn't come under an assumed name, because he left here when he was only five, and only an aunt survives. Cheer up, Lo! Even though the poetess should indeed prove to have murdered the dancer, if you can report at the same time that you have discovered that General Mo Te-ling has been wrongly executed, you'll stand a good chance of evading the impending crisis!'

'Good gracious, Dee, this is marvellous news! Tell me more about it while we are at table. It'll be an open-air affair, over there!'

He pointed at the open corridor running along the back of the terrace. Between the pillars stood tables, loaded with platters of cold snacks, alternating with piles of moon-cakes, artistically heaped into pyramids.

'I must leave now, Lo. I have to pay a visit downtown, then go on to the Black Fox Shrine. But I'll try to be back before your poetical gathering at four.'

After they had rejoined the others, the old lady intimated that she wanted to retire. The Academician and the others made their bows, and Lo and his First Lady led her inside. Judge Dee told the Academician that urgent papers had arrived by courier from Poo-yang, and asked to be excused from attending the open-air meal.

'Duty before pleasure. Off you go, Dee!'

XV

The judge went first to his own quarters, for he had to prepare his visit carefully. Relatives of a man executed for high treason, no matter how distant, are always mortally afraid of the authorities. Even after the lapse of many years, new evidence may come to light involving them in dangerous complications. He took a slip of red paper from the writing-box, and wrote SOONG LIANG on it in big letters. On the right he added 'Commission Agent', on the left an imaginary address in the city of Canton. Having changed into a plain blue cotton robe, and put a small black skull-cap on his head, he left the tribunal by the side gate.

On the street corner he found a small litter for hire. When he ordered the bearers to take him to Hwang's hardware shop, they protested that it was a long way, and to a poor district where the roads were bad. But after the judge had agreed to the fare without haggling, and added a generous tip in advance, they cheerfully carried him away.

The prosperous-looking shops in the main street reminded the judge of the fact that Hwang was in arrears with the payment of his fees to the guild. That meant the man must be desperately poor. He told the bearers to halt, and invested a silver piece in a large bolt of the best blue cotton. In the shop next door he bought two smoked ducks, and a box with moon-cakes. Having made these purchases, he continued his journey.

After the market they passed a residential quarter which the judge recognized as the ward where the tea-merchant Meng lived. Then they entered a quarter of the poor, crossed by narrow, smelly back streets, with irregular cobblestones. The half-naked children playing among the rubbish stopped to gape at the litter, a vehicle rarely seen in that neighbourhood. Not wanting to draw undue attention to his visit, the judge ordered the bearers to put him down in front of a small tea-house. One bearer could wait there by the litter, the other was to go on with him on foot, and carry the bolt of cloth and the basket with the ducks. The judge was glad he had taken the man, for soon they were in the midst of a veritable rabbit-warren of crooked alleys, where the bearer had to ask directions in the local dialect.

Hwang's shop consisted of an open street-stall, its patched canvas awning attached to the roof of a mud-brick shed behind. A row of cheap earthenware teapots hung on a cross-pole over a trestle table stacked with bowls and platters. Behind the improvised counter a broad-shouldered, shabbily dressed man was laboriously putting a dozen coppers on a string. When Judge Dee put the red card on the counter, the man shook his head. 'I can only make out the name Soong,' he said in a surly, coarse voice. 'What do you want?'

'My card says I am Soong Liang, a commission agent from Canton,' the judge explained. 'I am a distant cousin of your wife, you see. Came to look you up, on my way to the capital.'

Hwang's swarthy face lit up. Turning round to the woman sitting on the bench against the wall, bent over the needle-work in her lap, he called out, 'At last one of your relatives seems to have remembered you, woman! It's cousin Soong Liang, from Canton! Please come inside, sir, you've a long journey behind you!'

She quickly came to her feet. The judge ordered the bearer to hand her his purchases, then to wait for him in the street-stall opposite.

The hardware dealer took him into the small room that served as bed-sitting-room and kitchen. While Hwang quickly wiped the greasy table with a rag, the judge sat down on a bamboo stool and told the woman:

'Third Uncle wrote me from the capital that your parents

128

have died, cousin, but he gave me your address. Passing through here, I thought I'd drop in to offer you a few small gifts, for today's festival.'

She had opened the package and was looking with wide eyes at the bolt of cloth. He put her age at about forty. Her face was regular, but thin and deeply lined. Hwang exclaimed, startled:

'You're much too generous, cousin! Merciful Heaven, all that beautiful cloth! How could I ever return such a costly . . .'

'Simple! By allowing a lonely traveller to have his Mid-autumn meal with his own relatives! I brought a trifling contribution along.' He lifted the lid of the basket, and gave Hwang the box with moon-cakes. Hwang's eyes were on the contents of the basket.

'Two whole ducks! Cut them up carefully, woman! And take a new bowl and cups from the shop! I have saved a small jar of wine for today's festival, but I'd never have dreamed we'd have meat with it! And such expensive smoked duck!'

He poured the judge a cup of tea, then made polite inquiries about his guest's family in Canton, his business, and the journey he had behind him. Judge Dee told a convincing story, adding that he had to travel on that same afternoon. Then he said, 'We'll have one duck now; the other'll serve for tonight.'

Hwang raised his hand.

'Calamities of heaven and man may interfere between now and tonight, Cousin,' he declared solemnly. 'We'll eat our fill here and now!' He turned to his wife, who had been listening to the conversation with a pleased smile on her care-worn face. 'I promise, woman, that not one bad word about your family shall ever pass my lips again!' She gave the judge a shy look and said:

'After that terrible affair, Cousin, nobody dared to come to see us any more, you see.'

129

'The general's case was talked about even down south,' the judge remarked. 'It was very sad that your sister did away with herself before the disaster, but when you look at it from the broader point of view of our family's interest, it was all for the best. It saved us from being drawn into the affair.' As Hwang and his wife nodded ponderously, he asked, 'What happened to I-wen?'

Hwang sniffed. 'I-wen? Only heard a couple of years ago that he had become a man of letters. Far too snooty to remember his aunt!'

'Why did your sister do away with herself, Cousin? Was she treated badly in the general's house?'

'No, she wasn't,' the woman replied slowly. 'She was treated well, especially after she had borne I-wen, a sturdy, good-looking boy. But my sister was . . .'

'She was a blasted . . .' Hwang began. But his wife interrupted quickly: 'Mind your nasty tongue!' And to the judge: 'She couldn't help it, really. Perhaps it was Father's fault, after all . . .' She heaved a sigh and poured out the wine. 'Till she was fifteen she was a very quiet, obedient girl, you know, fond of animals. One day she came home with a small fox-baby she had found. When Father saw it, he became terribly afraid, for it was a black one, you see, a vixen. He killed it at once. Then my sister got a fit, and she was never the same afterwards.'

The hardware dealer gave the judge an uneasy look. 'That lewd fox-spirit went into her.'

His wife nodded. 'Father hired a Taoist priest, and he said many spells, but he couldn't get the fox-spirit out. When she was sixteen, she was making eyes at every young man in sight. Since she was a looker, mother had to keep an eye on her from morning till night. Then an old woman who peddled combs and powder in the big house told father that the First Lady of General Mo was looking for a concubine for the old master. Father was very glad, and when sister had

130

been taken to see the First Lady and she approved of sister, the deal was concluded. All went well; she had to work hard in the big house, but the First Lady gave her a new dress at each and every festival, and after she had borne I-wen, she wasn't beaten even once.'

'Had to spoil everything herself, the slut!' Hwang muttered. He hastily emptied his cup. His wife pushed a greying lock away from her forehead.

'One day I met the First Lady's maid in the market, and she said I was lucky to have a sister who didn't forget her own, who insisted on seeing her parents once every week. Then I knew there was something terribly wrong, for my sister hadn't come to see us for more than half a year. She did come afterwards, however. She was with child, and it wasn't the general's. I took her to a midwife who gave her all kinds of things to drink, but it didn't help. She bore a girl, told the general it had been a miscarriage, and had the child abandoned in the street.'

'That's what she was!' Hwang shouted angrily. 'A cruel, heartless fox-woman!'

'She was sorry she had to do it!' his wife protested. 'Wrapped the child up in a fine piece of brown Indian wool so that it wouldn't catch cold. That expensive saffron stuff, the Buddhists use to . . .' Seeing Judge Dee's startled face, she went on quickly, 'Sorry, Cousin, it's not a nice story at all! It's so long ago, but I still . . .' She began to weep.

Hwang patted her shoulder. 'Come on, no tears on this fine day!' And to the judge: 'We've no children ourselves, you see. Talking about it always gets her that way! Well, to cut a long story short, the old general found out, you see. One of his chair-coolies told us that the old man shouted he'd drag her and the fellow to the hall, and cut their heads off with his own sword! She hanged herself, and the general didn't get round to cutting off her lover's head, for the very next day the Emperor's soldiers came, and they cut off his

131

head! It's a strange world, Cousin! Let's have another drink. Here, you take one too, woman!'

'Who was her lover?' the judge asked.

'She never told me, Cousin,' the woman said, wiping her eyes. 'Only said he was a very learned gentleman who could go in and out of the big house.'

'Glad I chose the right sister!' Hwang shouted. His face had become flushed. 'My old woman works hard, takes in sewing and so we make both ends meet! But she doesn't know nothing about men's affairs, mind you! Wanted me to stop paying my fee to my guild! I says no, sell our winter clothes! If a man doesn't belong somewhere, he's nothing more than a stray dog! I was right there too, for that fine bolt of yours, Cousin, that'll keep us dressed up nicely for years to come! It's good for my business too, a well-dressed man behind the counter!'

After the judge had finished his rice, he told the woman: 'Take my card tomorrow to the back gate of the magistrate's residence, Cousin. I have done business with the housemaster, and he'll see to it that you get the sewing there.' He got up.

Hwang and his wife pressed him to stay, but he said he had to be in time for the ferry across the river.

The bearer took him back to the tea-house where the litter was waiting. He was carried back to the main street, his thoughts in a turmoil. Having paid the bearers off on the corner, he walked on to the tribunal. While the doorkeeper was admitting him by the side-gate, he learned from him that Magistrate Lo was in the ante-room, on the ground floor of the main building. Apparently the poetical gathering in the library had not yet started. The judge went quickly to his own courtyard.

He took from the drawer Lo's dossier on the case of the poetess. Standing at the table, he leafed through it till he found the text of the anonymous letter which had warned the magistrate that a dead body was buried under the cherry tree of the White Heron Monastery. Then he pulled the anonymous letter accusing General Mo Te-ling from his sleeve, and laid it beside the other. Slowly stroking his black beard, he compared the two. Both being chancery copies in the impersonal hand of clerks, the style had to show whether or not they could have been written by one and the same person. Doubtfully shaking his head, the judge put the two sheets in his sleeve, and went to the main courtyard.

The small magistrate was sitting at the tea-table, which was strewn with papers, a writing-brush in his hand, his lips pursed. He looked up and said eagerly:

'I am sifting out and correcting my recent work, Dee. Do you think the Academician would approve of the recurrent rhyme of this ballad?' He was going to recite the poem he had been correcting, but Judge Dee said quickly:

'Another time, Lo! I have a strange discovery to report.' He sat down opposite his colleague. 'I shall be brief, for you'll have to go presently to your library. It's getting on for four o'clock.'

'Oh, no, there's plenty of time, elder brother! The luncheon out in my fourth courtyard turned out to be a protracted affair, you know! The Court Poet and Yoo-lan wrote a few poems, and we discussed those, with lots of wine! All my four guests went straight to their rooms for a siesta, and none of them has shown up yet.'

'Good! So none of them went out, and so you needn't bother to mobilize your housemaster's agents to follow them. Now then, the mother of the murdered student was a concubine of General Mo Te-ling. Later she committed adultery with an unknown person, and their illegitimate daughter was abandoned. She's none other than Saffron, the guardian of the Black Fox Shrine.' Seeing Lo's astonished face, he raised his hand and went on, 'The abandoned child had been wrapped up in a piece of saffron wool, and people often call foundlings after the dress they had on when found. This

133

means that Saffron is Soong's half-sister, and that's why the student told Saffron he could never marry her. It also means that Saffron's father and the student's murderer are one and the same man. One day before the old general was arrested, he told his concubine that he had discovered she had committed adultery with one of his friends, adding that he would kill them both with his own hands. The concubine promptly hanged herself. And the general was arrested the next day, before he could settle with her lover.'

'Good gracious! Where did you find all that, Dee?'

'In your archives, mainly. The student Soong was evidently convinced that his mother's lover had falsely accused the general of high treason in an anonymous letter, to prevent the general from accusing him as an adulterer. Soong was wrong as to the first point. I read through the official record, and I am convinced the general was guilty. And his concubine's lover must have been in the plot. As to the second point, Soong was perfectly right. The man did write the anonymous letter, because he knew it would take the Censor some time to get round to the general, and he wanted to make sure that the general was arrested on the very first day of the investigation, so as to prevent him from taking action against him.'

Magistrate Lo raised his hand.

'Not so fast, Dee! If the general was guilty of high treason, why then should his denouncer have murdered the student? The chap had done a meritorious deed by informing against the general!'

'He must occupy a prominent position, Lo, and therefore he can't afford to have an adultery charge brought against him. Also, he evidently was deeply involved in the general's plot, else he wouldn't have known where the incriminating letters from the Ninth Prince were hidden. That's why he didn't come forward, although the government had promised him a reward.'

134

'Holy heaven! Who is the fellow, Dee?'

'I am afraid it must be one of your three guests, Shao, Chang or Loo. No, don't protest! I have irrefutable proof that it must be one of the three. Saffron shall tell us who. Even though her father kept his face covered when he visited her, I trust she'll be able to recognize him by his voice and general appearance.'

'You can't be serious about Sexton Loo, Dee! What woman would ever take that ugly man as a lover?'

'I am not so sure about that, Lo. The student's mother was a perverse woman. Her family ascribes that to her being possessed by the spirit of a lewd black vixen, by the way. However that may be, a perverse and frustrated woman— she was barely seventeen when she entered the general's house, and he getting on for sixty—might well have felt attracted to the sexton because of his very ugliness. Besides, he has a masterful and extraordinary strong personality, and many women are susceptible to such men. During the poetical gathering you might try to find out whether Chang and the sexton were here in Chin-hwa at the time of General Mo's trial, Lo. We know that the Academician was here, serving as Prefect of this area. Could you have your housemaster called?'

Lo clapped his hands, and gave an order to the boy servant. Judge Dee resumed:

'I would like you to find out also, Lo, whether any of our three suspects was in the Lake District this spring, at the time Yoo-lan was arrested in the White Heron Monastery.'

'Why do you want to know, Dee?' his colleague asked, astonished.

'Because in Yoo-lan's case too the authorities took action on the basis of an anonymous letter, written by a scholarly gentleman. And a criminal always likes to keep to one and the same method. In the case of General Mo's high treason the accusation was true; but by denouncing him the anonymous letter-writer achieved at the same time an ulterior purpose, namely preventing the general from taking action against him. Now, eighteen years later, the scholarly gentleman may well have again resorted to an anonymous letter to report another crime, namely the murder of the maidservant, and again to achieve some ulterior purpose. Therefore . . .' The judge broke off, for the housemaster came in.

Judge Dee took Lo's brush and jotted down on a scrap of paper the name and address of the hardware dealer Hwang, and the name Soong Liang. Handing it to the housemaster, he said, 'Mrs Hwang will come to the back door of the residence tomorrow morning, with the visiting-card of Mr Soong Liang. His Excellency wants you to see to it that she gets the sewing here. Detain her in conversation for a while, for we may want to see her. Now ask Mr Kao to come here.'

When the housemaster had left with a deep bow, Lo asked peevishly:

'Mr Soong Liang, you said? Who the hell is he?'

'It's me, as a matter of fact.' He gave his colleague a brief account of his visit to the hardware dealer, and concluded, 'They're a decent couple, and they have no children. I was toying with the idea of proposing to you that you entrust Saffron to them, after the poor girl has completely recovered. I must go to fetch her now, together with your counsellor.' Taking the two anonymous letters from his sleeve, he continued, handing them to Lo, 'These are chancery copies of the two anonymous letters. You are an expert on delicate nuances in literary style. Please have a good look at them, and see whether there's any indication of their having been composed by one and the same scholar. Put them in your sleeve, man! I see your counsellor coming!'

When the counsellor had made his bow, the small magistrate told him:

'I want you to accompany my colleague to the Black Fox Shrine, near the South Gate, Kao. I have decided to have that piece of wasteland cleaned up, and the first step is to get the half-witted woman away who acts as guardian of the shrine.'

'We shall go there together in an official palankeen, Mr Kao,' Judge Dee added. 'The house physician and the matron will follow us in a second, closed palankeen, for I have heard that the woman there is gravely ill.'

The counsellor bowed.

'I shall see to it at once, sir.' And to the magistrate: 'The Academician's boy servant is outside, Your Honour, with the message that His Excellency is now ready to receive his guests.'

'Holy heaven, my poems!' Lo exclaimed.

Judge Dee helped him to collect and sort out the papers strewn over the table. He accompanied his colleague to the second courtyard, then walked on alone to the tribunal.

Counsellor Kao was waiting for him at the gatehouse, where a large official palankeen stood ready.

'The physician and the matron are in that closed litter, sir,' he informed the judge. While they were being carried outside through the monumental arched gate, Kao resumed, 'The wasteland could be made into a public park, sir. It won't do to have right within our city walls an area where all kinds of ruffians can gather. Don't you agree, sir?'

'I do.'

'I hope you found in the archives what you were looking for this morning, sir.'

'I did.'

Perceiving that the judge was not in the mood for a leisurely conversation, Counsellor Kao kept silent. When they were passing through Temple Street, however, he began again:

'Yesterday morning I visited Sexton Loo in the temple at the end of this street, sir. I had quite some difficulty in persuading him to accept His Excellency's invitation. The sexton accepted only after I had told him you were a guest in the residence too.'

Judge Dee sat up.

'Did he say why?'

'He mentioned your great reputation as a criminal investigator, sir. And something about an interesting experiment, about foxes, if I remember correctly.'

'I see. Do you have any idea what he could've been referring to?'

'No, sir. The sexton is a very strange person. He seemed particularly keen on stressing he had arrived here the night before, but . . . Heavens, why are we halting here?' He looked outside.

The foreman of the bearers came up to the window, and reported to the counsellor:

'There's a crowd blocking the road, sir. Just one moment, please, I told them to make way.'

Judge Dee heard the confused noise of excited voices. Their palankeen went on for a while, then halted again. A sergeant of the guard appeared at the window. Saluting sharply, he told Kao:

'I am sorry, sir, but you had better not go on. The witch from the deserted temple has got the dog's madness. She . . .'

The judge quickly pulled the door-screen aside and stepped down from the palankeen. Six guards with levelled spears had formed a cordon across the street, keeping a small group of curious people away. Further down Saffron was lying sprawled on her back by the roadside, her still figure pitifully slight in the tattered, soiled robe. Two soldiers had pinned her neck down to the ground, with a forked thiefcatcher's stick ten feet long. A little further, in the middle of the empty road, other soldiers were lighting a bonfire.

'Better not come near, sir,' the sergeant warned Judge Dee. 'We're going to burn the dead body, to be quite sure. Don't know too much about how the sickness is transmitted.'

Counsellor Kao had come up to them. 'What happened, Sergeant?' he asked sharply. 'Is that woman dead?'

'Yes, sir. Half an hour ago, my men sitting in that street-stall heard wild screams from the brushwood over there, and a weird barking sound. Thinking that a mad dog was attacking someone, they rushed to the guardhouse, and we came back here with forked sticks. Just as I was about to enter that old gate there, the witch came running outside, screaming at the top of her voice. Her face was distorted something terrible, and there was foam coming from her mouth. She made for us, but one of my men caught her throat in the fork of his stick, and threw her on to the ground. She grabbed at the stick, thrashing about so violently that it needed a second man to keep her pinned down. At last her hands dropped away, and she was dead.' The sergeant pushed his iron helmet back and wiped his moist brow. 'What a wonderful man our magistrate is, sir! He must have been expecting something like this to happen! I got orders to post a few of my men in that stall there and keep an eye on the old gate. That's why we could be on the spot before she had attacked some of the passers-by.'

'Our magistrate is a deep one!' a soldier said with a grin.

Judge Dee beckoned the physician who had stepped down from the other litter.

'The dead woman had rabies,' he told him curtly. 'You agree the body should be burned?'

'Certainly, sir. Also the forked stick she was caught with. And the brushwood she came from had better be burned down too. It's a terrible disease, sir.'

'Stay here and see that everything is done properly,' the judge ordered Counsellor Kao. 'I am going back to the tribunal.'

XVI

A bevy of young maids was bustling about the three official palankeens that stood in the main courtyard of the residence. Some were putting brocade covers on the cushions, others were loading tea-baskets and boxes of sweetmeats. Their gay twitter jarred on Judge Dee's nerves. He went over to the housemaster. The greybeard was talking with the headman of the two-dozen palankeen bearers, who were squatting along the side-wall, neatly dressed in brown jackets with broad red sashes. The housemaster informed Judge Dee that the poetical meeting in the library was over. The guests had gone to their rooms to change, and Magistrate Lo had followed their example.

The judge went to his own quarters. He drew the armchair up in front of the open sliding-doors, and sat down wearily. Cupping his elbow in his left hand, he rested his chin on his tightly closed fist and stared sombrely at his rock garden, very quiet in the bleak sunshine of the late afternoon.

A long, drawn-out cry overhead made him raise his eyes. A flock of wild geese came flying over, their wings flapping leisurely in the blue sky. A sure sign of autumn.

At last he got up and went inside. Listlessly he changed into the same dark-violet robe he had worn the afternoon of the previous day. As he was placing the high cap of stiff black gauze on his head, he heard the clanging of iron boots in the front-yard. The military escort had arrived, which meant that the party would be leaving soon.

Crossing the main courtyard, he was joined by Loo. The sexton wore a faded blue gown, fastened round his ample waist by a straw rope, and large straw sandals on his bare feet. He was carrying a crooked stick, from which dangled a bundle of clothes. When the two men ascended the marble terrace in front of the main hall, where Magistrate Lo, the Academician and the Court Poet stood, resplendent in brocade robes, the sexton told them gruffly:

'Don't worry about my costume, gentlemen! I'll change in the temple on the cliff. This bundle contains my best robe.'

'You look impressive in any dress, Sexton!' the Academician told him genially. 'I'll ride with you, Chang. We must thrash out our differences over the poetical essay.'

'Go ahead!' the sexton said. 'I am going to walk.'

'Impossible, sir!' Magistrate Lo protested. 'The mountain road is steep, and . . .'

'I know the road well, and I've climbed steeper ones,' the sexton snapped. 'I like the mountain scenery, and the exercise. Just came here to tell you you needn't bother about transport for me.' He strode off, his crooked stick over his shoulder.

'Well, in that case I hope you'll ride with me, Dee,' Lo said. 'Miss Yoo-lan'll take the third palankeen, with my First Lady's chambermaid to look after her.' Turning to the Academician, he asked, 'May I lead you to the first palankeen, sir?'

The magistrate descended the marble steps with the Academician and the Court Poet, and the thirty soldiers presented their halberds. Just as Lo and Judge Dee were about to ascend the second palankeen, they saw the poetess appear on the terrace, an exquisite figure in a thin robe of white silk flaring out at her feet, and a long-sleeved blue brocade jacket with a silver flower motif. The mass of her hair was done up in an elaborate high coiffure, held in place with long silver hairneedles, their ends decorated with gold filigree pendants in which blue sapphires glittered. She was followed by an elderly maid in a plain blue gown.

Making himself comfortable in the cushions, Lo asked crossly:

'Did you see that dress and the hair-needles, Dee? She

141

borrowed them from my First Lady! Well, our poetical meeting didn't last very long. The Academician and Chang seemed a bit reluctant to give their candid opinion of my poetry. And the sexton didn't even try to hide his boredom! Unpleasant chap! Must say that Yoo-lan made a couple of very pertinent remarks. Fine feeling for language, the old girl has.' He turned up the points of his small moustache. 'Well, as to their whereabouts at the time of General Mo's trial, Dee, there I had no trouble at all. As soon as I had mentioned the case, the Academician promptly delivered a lecture on it. The Censor had summoned him for advice on the local situation, you see. As to Chang Lan-po, he was staying here too, for negotiations with discontented tenant farmers. The fellow's family owns about half the arable land in this district, you know. Chang attended the sessions of the tribunal, in order to observe conflicting human passions. That's what he said, at least. And Sexton Loo was staying in an old temple here, delivering a series of lectures on a Buddhist text. Didn't get around to asking them whether they were in the Lake District two months ago, when the poetess was arrested. Where did you put that girl from the Black Fox Shrine, Dee?'

'She's dead, Lo. From rabies. Must have got it from a fox. Was always fondling them, you know, even let them lick her face. And so . . .'

'Holy heaven, that's bad, Dee!'

'Very bad. For now we've no one to . . .' He broke off, for there was a loud clanging of gongs.

The palankeens had been carried from the residence to the tribunal, and had now arrived at the main gate of the compound. Twelve constables drew themselves up at the head of the cortège, four of them beating brass gongs. The others carried long stakes, with red-lacquered boards, some inscribed in golden letters with 'The Tribunal of Chin-hwa', others with 'Make way!' The rest had lanterns with the same inscrip-

142

tions, which would be lit when the party returned to the city that night.

The heavy, iron-bound main gate was pushed open, and the cortège moved out into the street. First the constables, next the three palankeens, escorted by ten soldiers on each side, and lastly ten soldiers, armed to the teeth, bringing up the rear. The milling crowd, dressed up for the feast, hastily made way for them. There were repeated shouts of 'Long live our magistrate!' Judge Dee noticed with satisfaction this further proof of his colleague's popularity in the district. After they had left the shopping street and it had become more quiet outside, the judge resumed:

'I had counted on Saffron to identify our man. Her death is a terrible blow, Lo. For I haven't a shred of proof. I do have proof, however, that it must have been one of your three guests. One of them must be Saffron's father, the same man murdered her half-brother, the student Soong—as I told you after my visit to Saffron's aunt. Now I can add that it was also the same man who murdered the dancer Small Phoenix.'

'Merciful heaven!' the magistrate shouted. 'That means that I . . .'

Judge Dee raised his hand.

'Unfortunately my discovery doesn't help you much as long as we can't prove who of the three is our man. Let me try to sum up the situation. The murder of the dancer Small Phoenix yesterday supplies a convenient starting-point. Then I shall take the murder of the student the day before yesterday, taking into account the background of General Mo's trial eighteen years ago. Finally we shall tackle together the murder of the maid in the White Heron Monastery. In this manner we shall be able to see all these problems in the correct chronological setting.

'Well, to begin with the murder of the dancer. The crucial point is that Small Phoenix had seen Saffron's father on the wasteland, when he was on the way back from a visit to his

143

daughter. The meeting did not mean anything to the dancer at that time, for she had never seen the man before. Yesterday afternoon Small Phoenix wanted to have a look at your banquet hall where she was going to perform in the evening, and Yoo-lan, who was enamoured of her, took her along to your residence. She had told the poetess that she was going to perform "A Phoenix among Purple Clouds", which she considered her best number. Then she met your three guests. It was that brief meeting, Lo, that made the dancer suddenly decide to change her programme. She dropped the plan for the Purple Cloud dance which she knew so well and which always made a hit with the audience, and changed to the "Black Fox Lay"—which she had never performed in public before, and of which she didn't even have a good musical score!'

'By heaven!' Lo shouted. 'The wench had recognized the man she met on the wasteland!'

'Exactly! She had recognized him, but he had given no sign of recognizing her. Well, she would jog his memory! The Black Fox Dance would remind him! After her dance, when she would sit for a while with each of the guests for a cup of wine, as is customary, she would tell him she knew he was Saffron's father, and make her demands. Since she was an ambitious girl devoted to her art, I assume that in the case of Shao or Chang, she would ask to be introduced into the highest circles of the capital, probably adding a demand for a substantial monthly income. And in the case of the sexton, insist that he constitute himself her patron, adopt her as his daughter, for instance, and put all the weight of his great name behind her artistic career. Blackmail, pure and simple.'

The judge stroked his beard, and continued with a sigh:

'She was a clever girl, but she had underestimated her victim. As soon as he had recognized her, he began to plan her removal. Your announcement that she was going to dance to the "Black Fox Lay", a clear warning that she had recognized him as the visitor to the wasteland, and that she meant business, made him decide to murder her as soon as a suitable opportunity presented itself. The interval of the fireworks supplied that opportunity, and he utilized it. In the manner I explained to you last night. It is on the basis of this reasoning, Lo, that I maintain I have irrefutable proof that one of your three guests is the murderer.'

'Am I glad that Yoo-lan didn't do it!' the magistrate exclaimed. 'It's true that we don't know which of the three did do it, but you have saved my career, elder brother! For now I can report the dancer's murder in good conscience as a local affair that had nothing to do with the poetess! I'll never be able to repay you for this, I . . .'

He was interrupted by shouted commands and the clatter of arms. The cortège was passing outside through the west city gate. Judge Dee began quickly:

'Second, the murder of the student Soong. He was a child of five at the time of his father's trial, and was taken to the capital at once, by an uncle. We can only guess when and how he obtained data which convinced him his father had been falsely accused. I presume he knew the story of his mother's adultery; his uncle or another relative must have told him that after he had grown up, for his aunt said he had never visited her here in Chin-hwa. Somehow or other he must have discovered that Saffron was the issue of the adulterous liaison, and that's why he came here and established contact with his half-sister. At the same time he searched the records in your archives for the details of his father's trial. Saffron had not told him she had a father who came to see her occasionally, but she must have told her father about the student. That his name was Soong I-wen, that he had come to Chin-hwa to bring his father's murderer to justice, and that he was staying with the tea-merchant Meng. The criminal went to Merchant Meng's house, and killed Soong.'

The small magistrate nodded eagerly.

'Then he searched Soong's lodgings, Dee, looking for eventual notes that might give a clue to his own identity. Perhaps he did find old letters of General Mo, or of his mother. The authorities had confiscated all the general's property, but the family will have taken one or two robes, and many years later the student may have discovered confidential papers sewn into the lining, or heaven knows what!'

'That, Lo, we shall know only when we have identified the murderer, and collected sufficient evidence to question him. But I can't see a ghost of a chance that we ever will, for the moment! Before going into that problem, however, I want to discuss my third point, namely the case pending against the poetess, for having allegedly whipped to death her maid in the White Heron Monastery. Tell me, what did you make of those two anonymous letters I gave you?'

'Not much, Dee. Both were composed by a good scholar, and you know how strict the rules of our literary style are. There is a fixed expression for every conceivable aspect or contingency of human life, thought, and action, and every scholar will use exactly the right phrase in exactly the right place. If the letters had been written by an uneducated person, it would have been different, of course. Then it's easy to pick out similar mannerisms, or similar mistakes. As it is, I can only say one notices a resemblance in the use of some prepositions, that might suggest both letters had been written by the same man. Sorry, Dee!'

'Wish I could see those letters in the original!' Judge Dee exclaimed. 'I have made a close study of handwriting, and I am sure I would then know for certain! But that would necessitate a journey to the capital. And I doubt whether the Metropolitan Court would allow me to inspect the letters!' Vexedly he tugged at his moustache.

'Why do you need to know about the letters, Dee? With your sharp eyes, elder brother, you must have other means of deciding which of my three guests is the murderer! Heavens, the fellow must have been leading a double life! You must have caught something in their talk, or in their . . .'

Judge Dee shook his head emphatically.

'Not a hope, Lo! Our basic problem is that all three are extraordinary men, whose actions and reactions cannot be gauged by ordinary means. Let's admit it, Lo! These three men are our betters in learning, talent and experience—not to speak of the prominent position they occupy in our national life! Questioning them directly would be courting disaster, both for you and for me. And to try to get at them indirectly by the normal tricks of our trade would be of no avail. These are men of superlative intellectual attainments, my friend, self-possessed people, wise to the ways of the world! And the Academician, for one, has had longer experience as a criminal investigator than you or me! Trying to bluff them, or to startle them into an unguarded word, is just so much labour lost!'

Lo shook his head. He said disconsolately:

'To tell you the truth, Dee, I can't yet get accustomed to the idea that one of these three great writers is a murder suspect. How could you possibly explain such a man committing brutal, callous crimes?'

Judge Dee shrugged his shoulders.

'We can only make rough guesses. I could imagine, for instance, that the Academician is suffering from a surfeit of experience. Having had all that normal life has to offer, he seeks for abnormal sensations. The Court Poet, on the contrary, labours visibly under the impression that he has only lived on second-hand emotions, and that therefore his poetry is no good. And a feeling of frustration may engender the most unexpected actions. As to Sexton Loo, you told me that before his conversion to the new creed he cruelly oppressed his monastery's tenant farmers. And now he has apparently chosen to place himself beyond good and evil, and that is a very dangerous attitude to take. I just mention a few simple explanations that come to mind, Lo. It's doubtless much more complicated than that!'

The small magistrate nodded. He opened one of the baskets, took a handful of sweetmeats, and began to munch them. Judge Dee wanted to pour himself a cup of tea from the tea-basket under the seat but the palankeen began to list backwards at a sharp angle. He drew the window-curtain open. They were ascending a steep mountain road, lined by tall pine trees. Lo delicately wiped his hands on his handkerchief and resumed:

'Routine checks aren't any use either, Dee. As regards Shao and Chang, at least. Both told me they had gone to bed early the day before yesterday when the student was murdered. Now you know that the government hostel where they stayed is a big and busy place; all kinds of officials are going in and out there at all times. Impossible to check their movements. Especially since either of them will have taken good care he wasn't noticed when he slipped out late at night! How about the sexton, though?'

'Just as bad. Anyone can enter or leave that temple, as I found out myself. And there's a short cut from there to the quarter near the East Gate, where the tea-merchant lives. Now that Saffron is gone, I greatly fear that we have come to a dead end, Lo.'

The two magistrates sank into a morose silence. Judge Dee let his sidewhiskers slowly glide through his fingers. After a long pause he said suddenly:

'Just now I went over last night's dinner party again in my mind. Didn't it strike you, Lo, how very nicely your guests behaved to each other? All four of them, including the poetess? Courteous but reserved, friendly but impersonal, and with just that touch of light banter one expects among a small gathering of colleagues in letters, each of whom has reached the top in his particular field. Yet these four people have been seeing each other on and off for a number of years. Who knows what they really think about each other, what memories of mutual or shared love or hatred bind them? None of the three men will ever give as much as a hint of their real emotions. The poetess, however, is another proposition. She's by nature a passionate woman, and the six weeks in prison and the trials have put her under a heavy strain. Last night she lifted one tip of her mask. Only once, but I felt a definite tension in the air, for one brief moment.'

'You mean after she had recited that strange poem on "The Happy Reunion"?'

'Precisely. She likes you, Lo, and I am firmly convinced she would never have composed the poem if she hadn't been in such a state of emotional tension that she simply forgot you were there. Later, when we were watching the fireworks on the balcony, and when she had calmed down, she more or less apologized to you. The poem was meant for one of your three guests, Lo.'

'I am glad to hear that,' the small magistrate said dryly. 'I was really shocked by her violent denunciation. Especially since the poem was damned good, for an improvisation on the spot.'

'What did you say? I am sorry, Lo, I was thinking again about those two anonymous letters. If they were written by the same man, it means that one of your guests hates Yoo-lan. Hates her so deeply that he wants to bring her to the scaffold. Again we come back to the crucial question: which of the three is it? Well, I promised you I would discuss the White Heron case with the poetess. I hope that tonight I shall have an opportunity. Then I shall broach the subject of the anonymous letter, and unobtrusively watch their reactions, especially those of the poetess. I must tell you frankly, however, that I don't expect much of that attempt!'

'A cheerful thought!' the magistrate muttered. He leaned back into the cushions, and resignedly folded his hands over his paunch.

149

After some time they came on to level ground again. The palankeen halted amidst the noise of confused voices.

They were on a stretch of table land, in an open space among the huge old pine trees whose deep, bluish-green colour had given the Emerald Cliff its name. Further ahead, on the very edge of the cliff, stood a single-storeyed pavilion, open on all four sides, the heavy roof supported by stately rows of thick wooden pillars. The cliff was overhanging a deep mountain gorge. Opposite rose two mountain ranges, the first ridge about level with the pavilion, the second towering into the red-streaked sky. At the other end of the cliff was a small temple, its pointed roof half hidden by the high branches of the pine trees. In front of the temple stood a cluster of small food-stalls, closed now because of the magistrate's visit. Lo's cooks had established there an open-air kitchen. Servants carrying hampers and large wine-jars were busy about the trestle tables put up under the trees. It was there that all the constables, guards and other officers of the tribunal would be entertained. The chair-bearers and coolies would take care of the rest of the food and the wine.

When Magistrate Lo was standing by the first palankeen to welcome the Academician and the Court Poet, the dishevelled figure of Sexton Loo came into sight. He had tucked the slips of his faded blue gown under his straw belt, revealing his muscular, hairy legs. He carried the clothes bundle over his shoulder on the crooked stick, as peasants do.

'You look like a real mountain recluse, Sexton!' the Academician shouted. 'But one who thrives on better things than just pine-seeds and morning dew!'

The obese monk grinned, revealing his brown, uneven teeth. He went off in the direction of the temple. Magistrate Lo conducted his other guests up a path strewn with pine-needles, leading to the granite steps of the slightly raised base of the pavilion. Judge Dee, who was bringing up the rear, noticed that three soldiers had not followed the others to the improvised kitchen. They were squatting together under a tall pine tree, about half-way between the pavilion and the temple. They wore spiked iron helmets, and had their swords strapped to their backs. He recognized the broad-shouldered sergeant he had seen in the tribunal: they were the guards, the Prefect's escort of the poetess. Magistrate Lo's guarantee for the poetess only covered her stay in the residence. Now that she was outside, her escort was on the alert again. They were right, for they were answerable for the prisoner with their lives. But their grim presence at this gay excursion gave the judge a sudden pang of anxiety.

XVII

Judge Dee followed the others into the pavilion. They had a
quick cup of hot tea, then Magistrate Lo took them to the
low balustrade of carved marble that marked the edge of the
cliff. Standing there at the balustrade, they silently watched
the red disc of the sun sink behind the mountains. Then the
shadows gathered quickly over the gorge. Bending over, Judge
Dee saw that there was a sheer drop of more than a hundred
feet. A thin mist came up from the mountain stream that
swirled over the jagged rocks, deep down below.

The Court Poet turned round.

'An unforgettable sight!' he said reverently. 'Wish I could
capture its magnificence in a few lines, evoking . . .'

'As long as you don't copy mine!' the Academician interrupted with a thin smile. 'The first time I visited this famous
site—I was accompanying the State Counsellor Chu—I
wrote four stanzas on this sunset. The Counsellor had them
engraved on the rafters here, I suppose. Let's have a look,
Chang!'

They all went to inspect the dozens of larger and smaller
boards hanging from the pavilion's rafters, all bearing essays
and poems composed by famous visitors. The Academician
told the waiter who was lighting the floor-lamps to hold one
high. Peering up, the Court Poet exclaimed:

'Yes, Shao, there is your poem! Very high up, but I can
still make out the text. Fine classic style!'

'I hobble along on the crutches of old quotations,' the
Academician said. 'They might have given it a better place,
though. Ah, yes, now I remember! On that occasion the
counsellor bestowed on our meeting the name of "Gathering

above the Clouds". Does anyone have a good suggestion for tonight's meeting?'

' "The Gathering in the Mist".' A hoarse voice spoke up. It was Sexton Loo who had come up the steps, now clad again in his long wine-red robe with the black borders.

'Very good!' the Court Poet called out. 'There's indeed a great deal of mist. Look at those long trailers drifting among the trees!'

'I was not referring to that,' the sexton remarked.

'Let's hope the moon'll be out soon,' Judge Dee said. 'The Mid-autumn Festival is devoted to the moon!'

The servants had filled the wine cups on the round, red-lacquered table standing close by the marble balustrade. It was loaded with platters of cold dishes. The small magistrate raised his cup.

'I respectfully bid all of you welcome to the Gathering in the Mist! Since this is a very simple, rustic meal, I propose that we all sit down without regard to the conventionalities!'

He was careful, however, to offer the Academician the seat on his right, and the poet the one on his left. There was a chill in the air, but thick padded quilts had been draped over the chairs, and wooden foot-rests placed on the paved floor. Judge Dee sat down opposite his colleague, between Sexton Loo and the poetess. The waiters put large bowls with piping hot dumplings on the table. Lo's chief cook had evidently realized that the guests wouldn't care for too many preliminary cold dishes on this chilly night up on the cliff. Two maids refilled the cups. The sexton emptied his in one draught, then said in his croaking voice:

'I had a fine climb. Saw one gold pheasant, and two gibbons swinging in the trees. Also a fox. A very large one. It . . .'

'I do hope you'll spare us your spooky fox-stories tonight, Sexton!' the poetess interrupted with a smile. And to the judge: 'Last time we met in the Lake District, he gave all of

153

us goose-flesh!' Judge Dee thought she was looking much better than at noon. But that might be because of her elaborate make-up.

The sexton fixed her with his bulging eyes.

'I have second sight, at times,' he said quietly. 'If I tell others what I see, it's partly to show off, partly to allay my own fears. For I don't like the things I see. Personally, I prefer to look at animals. In the wild.'

It struck Judge Dee that the sexton was in an unusually subdued mood.

'At my former post, Han-yuan,' the judge remarked, 'there were many gibbons in the forest, just behind my residence. I watched them every day while having my morning tea on the back gallery.'

'It's a good thing to like animals,' the sexton said slowly. 'One never knows what animal one was in a former existence. Neither into what animal one's soul might migrate in a future incarnation.'

'I imagine you were a fierce tiger once, Magistrate!' the poetess told Judge Dee archly.

'A watchdog rather, madam!' the judge said. And to the sexton: 'Well, sir, you stated you aren't a Buddhist any more. Yet you believe in the doctrine of transmigration.'

'Of course I do! Why do some people live in abject misery from cradle to grave? Or why does a young child die a painful and horrible death? The only acceptable explanation is that they expiate sins committed during a former life. How could the Powers on High expect us to make amends for all the wrongs we do in only one single lifetime?'

'No, no, I insist, Lo!' the voice of the Academician cut into their conversation. 'You must recite one of your naughty love poems! To prove your reputation as a great lover!'

'Lo is a lover of love,' the poetess remarked dryly. 'He dallies with many, because he lacks the capacity to really love one.'

'An unkind remark to our worthy host!' the Court Poet called out. 'As a fine, you shall recite one of your own love poems, Yoo-lan!'

'I don't recite love poetry. Not any more. But I'll write one verse for you.' Magistrate Lo beckoned the housemaster and pointed at the side-table where ink and paper had been made ready. Judge Dee noticed that his colleague had grown pale. Yoo-lan's remark had apparently touched a raw spot. The housemaster was selecting a sheet of paper, but the Academician shouted:

'Our great Yoo-lan shan't write her immortal verse on a scrap of paper! Write on the pillar there, so that your poem can be engraved in the wood, to be read and admired by later generations!'

The poetess shrugged. She got up and went to the nearest pillar. One maidservant followed her with a square inkslab and a writing-brush, another stood by with a candle. Yoo-lan rubbed the pillar till she found a smooth space. Again the judge was struck by her slender, expressive hands. She moistened the brush on the inkslab and wrote in clear, elegant characters:

> Bitterly I search for the right words,
>> For this poem, written under my lamp.
> I cannot sleep the long night,
>> Fearing the lonely coverlets.
> In the garden outside
>> Is the soft rustling of the autumn leaves.
> The moon shines forlornly
>> Through the gauze window panes.

'Ha!' the Academician exclaimed. 'All the nostalgic mood of autumn captured in four lines. Our poetess is forgiven! Let's all drink to her!'

They had many more rounds, while the waiters served new hot dishes. Four large copper braziers heaped with glowing coals had been placed at the four corners of the company, for now that night had fallen it was becoming cold on the cliff, and a damp mist was rising up from the gorge. Dark clouds obscured the moon. Magistrate Lo, who had been staring absent-mindedly at the glow of the lampions in the pine trees outside, now suddenly leaned forward.

'What the devil are those three soldiers making a fire for, there under the trees?'

'Those are my guards, Magistrate,' the poetess told him evenly.

'The impudent rascals!' Lo shouted. 'I shall have them immediately . . .'

'Your guarantee covers only my stay inside your residence,' she reminded him quickly.

'Ah . . . hm. Yes, I see,' Lo muttered. Then he asked sharply: 'Where's the sweet-sour carp, Housemaster?'

Judge Dee personally refilled Yoo-lan's cup, and told her:

'My friend Lo gave me his notes on the case that is pending against you, madam. He thought I might be able to help you draw up your plea. I am not a very good writer, but I have made a special study of legal documents, and . . .'

The poetess put her cup down.

'I do appreciate the kind intention, sir. But six weeks in various prisons gave me ample time to consider the merits of my case. Although I lack as a matter of course your immense knowledge of legal phraseology, I still think that I myself am the person best qualified for drawing up my defence. Let me pour you another drink!'

'Don't be a fool, Yoo-lan!' the sexton said brusquely. 'Dee has made quite a reputation for himself in the field!'

'It struck me,' Judge Dee resumed, 'that the fact that the case was initiated on the basis of an anonymous letter was not given its full weight. I could find no indication of anyone going into the question of how the writer came to know about the buried body. The letter was written by an accom-

156

苦吟搜詩堦下吟
不眠長夜

THE POETESS INSCRIBES A PILLAR

plished scholar, which rules out the members of the robber band. Don't you have any idea about his identity, madam?'

'If I had,' she replied curtly, 'I would have told the judges.' She emptied her cup, then added: 'Or maybe not.'

There was a sudden silence. Then the Court Poet remarked dryly:

'Inconsistency is the privilege of a beautiful and talented woman. I drink to you, Yoo-lan!'

'I join that toast!' the Academician boomed. There was general laughter, but the judge thought it didn't ring true. All had been drinking heavily, but he knew that the three men had a tremendous capacity, and they gave not the slightest sign of losing their composure. But there was a feverish glint in the eyes of the poetess; she seemed on the verge of breaking down. He must try to draw her out further, for her enigmatic last remark seemed to imply that she suspected someone, and that the person she suspected was sitting here at this table.

'The anonymous letter accusing you, madam,' he resumed, 'reminded me of one written here in Chin-hwa eighteen years ago. The letter that brought about the downfall of General Mo Te-ling. That letter had also been written by an accomplished scholar, you see.'

She darted a sharp look at him. Raising her curved eyebrows, she asked:

'Eighteen years ago, you say? That doesn't seem very helpful to me!'

'The fact is,' Judge Dee went on, 'that I met here a person who was connected with the general's case. Indirectly, it's true. Yet our conversation opened interesting possibilities. It was the daughter of one of the general's concubines. Of the surname Soong.'

He looked round at the sexton. But the obese monk didn't seem to have followed the conversation; he was intent on his food, a vegetarian dish of stewed bamboo shoots. The Acade-

158

mician and the Court Poet were listening, but their faces betrayed only polite interest. Out of the corner of his eye he saw the startled look on the face of the poetess by his side. Amazed, he made a quick calculation: she had been only twelve at that time! Apparently someone had told her about the case. Someone who knew. The sexton put down his chopsticks.

'Soong, you say? Wasn't that the name of the student who was murdered here the other day?'

'Indeed, sir. It was in connection with that murder that my colleague and I went into that old case of General Mo's high treason.'

'Don't know what you were trying to find there, of course.' The Academician joined the conversation. 'But if you think there was something wrong with the verdict on the general, Lo, you're barking up the wrong tree! I acted as the Censor's adviser, you know; followed the whole trial closely. And I can tell you that the man was guilty. A pity, for he was a good soldier. Outwardly a genial kind of chap, too. But the core was rotten. Had been brooding over a matter of promotion.'

The Court Poet nodded. He took a sip from his cup and said in his precise voice:

'I know next to nothing about judicial affairs, Lo, but I am interested in puzzles. Could you explain what the connection is between that old trial for high treason, and the recent murder of this student?'

'The murdered student's name being Soong, sir, we thought he might be a half-brother of the concubine's daughter my colleague Dee mentioned just now.'

'That seems to me nothing but a wild guess!' the poet protested.

Yoo-lan wanted to speak, but Judge Dee said quickly:

'Oh no, sir. The general's concubine had abandoned her daughter, you see, because it was the issue of an adulterous relationship. We reasoned that when the student learned that

159

his half-sister was living here, and also her mother's lover, he might have come to Chin-hwa to look for that man. For my colleague and I found out that the student visited the archives in the tribunal here in order to make a study of the general's friends and relations.'

'My compliments, Lo!' the Academician shouted. 'While entertaining us so lavishly, you managed to go about your official duties at the same time! And so quietly that we didn't even suspect it! Any clue to the murderer of the student?'

'It was my colleague Dee who did all the real work, sir! He can tell you about the latest developments.'

'By a mere chance,' the judge said, 'I located Soong's half-sister. She's the guardian of the Black Fox Shrine at the South Gate, as a matter of fact. She's a half-wit, but . . .'

'A mentally deranged person's evidence is not admitted in court,' the Court Poet interrupted. 'Even I do know that much about legal affairs!'

The sexton had turned round in his chair. Fixing the judge with his protruding eyes, he asked:

'So you know Saffron, eh, Dee?'

XVIII

Sexton Loo pursed his thick lips. Turning his wine cup round in his large, hairy hand, he resumed pensively:

'I visited that girl too, once. Am interested in her because she has a definite affinity with foxes, you see. Place is crawling with them. Know her background? She was sold to a cheap brothel, but bit off the tongue of her first customer. Fox-like gesture, that! Effective too, for the fellow nearly bled to death, and in the confusion she jumped out of the window, and made straight for the fox shrine on the wastelands. Has been there ever since.'

'When did you see her last, sir?' Judge Dee asked casually.

'When? Oh, must have been about a year or so ago. When I came back here three days ago I wanted to spend more time with her. In order to find out exactly what the tie is between her and those foxes.' He shook his large head. 'Went there a couple of times, but turned back at the entrance gate of the wasteland each time. Because of the large crowd of spectres about there.' He refilled his cup. Turning to Magistrate Lo, he resumed, 'That girl you hired to dance for us last night also had a foxy look, Lo. How's her foot coming along?'

The small magistrate shot Judge Dee a questioning look. When the judge nodded, Lo said to the company in general:

'We didn't want to distress you last night, gentlemen, so you were informed she had an accident. In fact, she was murdered.'

'I knew it!' the sexton muttered. 'Her dead body was lying there close by us, all the time we were drinking and talking.'

The Court Poet had been looking dumbfounded at Yoo-lan. 'Murdered?' he asked. 'And you found her?'

As the poetess nodded, the Academician said crossly:

'Should've told us, Lo! We aren't so easily distressed, you know. And with my long experience as investigating judge, I might have given you a useful hint or two. Well, so you have two murders on your hands, eh? Any clue to the scoundrel who did the dancer in?'

Seeing that his colleague hesitated, Judge Dee replied in his stead:

'Both cases are narrowly connected, sir. As regards the student Soong and the research he was conducting here, I fully agree with you that his father had indeed been guilty of high treason, and that in this respect the student was barking up the wrong tree. But my colleague and I think that the student was well on the way to tracking down the person who had denounced his father, not for a patriotic, but for a most selfish reason, namely . . .' He was interrupted by a startled cry from the poetess.

'Must you go on with all that horrible talk?' she asked in a trembling voice. 'With this sly stalking of your prey, closing in, in ever narrowing circles. . . . Have you forgotten that I am also an accused, with a death sentence hanging over my head? How can you . . .'

'Steady, Yoo-lan!' the Academician intervened. 'You haven't to worry about anything! There's not the slightest doubt about your acquittal, of course. The judges of the Metropolitan Court are excellent men, I know them all. I can assure you that they'll hear your case as a mere formality, then summarily dismiss it.'

'Absolutely,' the Court Poet said. Judge Dee resumed quickly:

'I have good news for you, madam. I said a few minutes ago that the anonymous letter denouncing General Mo, and the one accusing you, were both written by a good scholar. Now we have found out that the writer must have been one and the same person. That opens up a new line of approach to your case, madam.'

162

The Academician and the Court Poet looked at the judge in blank astonishment.

'Let's have more about the murder of the foxy dancer,' the sexton croaked. 'Happened in the room next door to ours, after all!'

'Indeed, sir. You're familiar, of course, with the story of the Consort's Staircase. And with the fact that the consort of the Ninth Prince utilized the door behind the screen in the banquet hall to . . .' There was a loud crash at Judge Dee's side.

The poetess had jumped up, overturning her chair. Looking down at the judge with flaming eyes, she shouted at him:

'You utter fool! You with your far-fetched, fumbling theories! You can't even see the simple truth right before your eyes!' She pressed her hands against her heaving bosom, in a frantic attempt to regain her breath. 'I tell you I am sick and tired of all this pettifoggery. I've had nearly two months of it, I can't stand it any longer! I am through!' Hitting her fist on the table, she screamed, 'It was me who killed that blackmailing dancer, you fool! She was asking for it! Stuck the scissors into her scrawny neck, then went to you and acted my part!'

There was a deep silence while she surveyed the company with her burning eyes. Judge Dee looked up at her, dumbfounded.

'That's the end!' Magistrate Lo muttered.

Then the poetess lowered her eyes. She resumed, calmer now:

'The student Soong had been my lover. I know he was obsessed by the idea that his father had been falsely accused. The dancer told me that Soong went to see Saffron. A poor half-wit, suffering from erotic hallucinations. Keeps a skeleton dressed up in a shroud as her lover. Smarting under the fact that she's a foundling, she dreamed up a father who came to

163

see her regularly. Small Phoenix told me, said she fortified Saffron in that illusion, just to keep her in a good mood so she would teach her those weird songs. I tell you that Small Phoenix was a sly, malicious bitch who fully deserved to die. She had wormed my secret out of Soong. That's what she wanted to blackmail me with, as I found out yesterday afternoon. She was going to dance the "Purple Cloud", but after she had met me and thought over her chances, she changed to the "Black Fox Lay". As a gentle hint to me that she had met Soong out there in the ruined temple.'

She had been talking so fast that she had to stop again, gasping for breath. Judge Dee tried frantically to sort out the confused statement. His carefully built-up case was crumbling to pieces before he had even begun to formulate it. There was a clanging of iron. The three guards, alerted by the crash of the chair and the shouting of the poetess, had come to the pavilion. The sergeant stood at a pillar, surveying the scene with a dubious look. The others didn't see him. All eyes were on the poetess who was standing there, her hands on the table. Then Judge Dee asked in a voice he hardly recognized as his own:

'What was your secret the dancer learned from Soong?'

The poetess turned round and beckoned the sergeant.

'Come here, Sergeant! You've treated me decently, and you've a right to hear this!' As the sergeant came up to the table, casting a worried glance at Magistrate Lo, the poetess resumed:

'Soong had been my lover, but soon I was through with him and sent him away. Last autumn, that was. Six weeks ago, he stayed for a few days in the Lake District. Came to see me and implored me to take him back. I refused. I've had my fill of lovers. I had come to hate men, had only a few girl friends left. For what they were worth! I discovered that my maid had deceived me with a coolie, and I sent her packing. She came back later that night, thinking that I had left already for my evening walk. I caught her while she was emptying my jewel box.'

She paused, impatiently pushing away a lock that had strayed to her brow from her sagging coiffure.

'I wanted to give her a good whipping. But then . . . then it wasn't her I was whipping, each and every lash was aimed at me myself, at my incredible, my stupid folly! When I came to myself and realized what I was doing, she was lying there, dead. I dragged her body to the garden, and found Soong standing by the back gate. Without saying a word he helped me carry her to the cherry tree, and bury her there. When he had levelled the ground, he spoke up. Told me that we would keep the secret—together. I said never. That by helping me to conceal the body he had become an accomplice to murder, and that he better make himself scarce. He slunk away. I thought I had to protect myself in case the body should ever be found, and forced the lock of the garden gate. The two silver candlesticks I buried under the altar in the chapel.'

She heaved a deep sigh. Turning again to the sergeant, she said softly:

'I offer you my apologies. You discreetly waited outside when I went into the silver shop here three days ago. There I ran into Soong. He whispered to me that now that his anonymous letter was apparently insufficient to bring me to the scaffold, he was going to take other measures. But perhaps I'd like to talk things over with him first. I promised I would visit him at midnight. Out of consideration for me, Sergeant, you hadn't posted one of your men at the door of my room. I slipped out of the inn, and went to Soong's lodging. After he had let me inside, I killed him. With a compass saw I had picked up from the rubbish heap in the alley. Well, that's all.'

'I am very sorry, madam,' the sergeant said. With an impassive face he began to unwind the thin chain he carried round his waist.

'You were always good at improvising on the spot.' A deep voice spoke. It was the Academician. He had got up and now stood there behind his chair, an impressive figure, tall and broad in his flowing brocade robe. The light of the lampions hanging from the eaves fell on his haughty, set face, the pupils very large against the white of his rolling eyes. He carefully straightened his robe, then said casually, 'However, I don't want to owe anything to a common whore.'

Without apparent haste he stepped over the low balustrade.

The poetess began to scream, high, piercing screams. Judge Dee jumped up and sprang to the balustrade, with the sergeant and Sexton Loo close behind him. From the darkness deep down below came only the faint sound of the stream gushing through the gorge.

When Judge Dee turned away, Yoo-lan's screams had stopped. She stood there at the balustrade, stunned, beside the Court Poet. Magistrate Lo was issuing quick orders to the housemaster. The greybeard nodded and rushed down the steps. The poetess went back to the table. Sitting down heavily she said in a toneless voice:

'He was the only man I ever loved. Let's have a last drink together. Soon I'll have to say good-bye. Look, the moon has come out!'

When they were seated at the table again, the sergeant stepped back and stood himself against the farthest pillar. His two men joined him there. While Judge Dee silently refilled Yoo-lan's cup, Magistrate Lo said:

'According to my housemaster, there's a footpath farther on, leading down into the ravine. A few of my men are going down there now, to look for the body. But it'll probably be found a mile or so downstream, for the current is very fast.'

The poetess put her elbows on the table. She said with a wan smile:

'Years ago already he had elaborate drawings made for a magnificent mausoleum, to be erected in his native place, after his death. And now his body . . .' She buried her face in her hands. Lo and the sexton looked in silence at her shaking shoulders. The Court Poet had averted his face; he was staring at the moonlit mountain range, his eyes wide. Then she let her hands drop.

'Yes, he was the only man I really loved. I liked the poet Wen Tung-yang, he was generous, and good company. And a few others. But Shao Fan-wen was here, right inside me, under my skin. I fell in love with him when I was nineteen. He made me secretly leave the house I was working in, refused to buy me out. When he was through with me, he left me without a penny. I had to making a living as a cheap whore, for, having fled from the house in the capital, my name was on the black list, so that I couldn't enter any high-class establishment anywhere. I fell ill, nearly starved. He knew, but he couldn't have cared less. Later, after Wen Tung-yang had put me on my feet again, I tried to get him back, several times. He shoved me out of his way, as one pushes away an over-affectionate dog. Did he make me suffer! And I never ceased to love him.'

She emptied her cup in one draught. Giving Magistrate Lo a pitiful look, she resumed:

'When you invited me to stay with you, Lo, I said no at first, because I thought I would never want to see him again . . . hear that pompous voice again, see that . . .' She shrugged. 'But when you really love a man, you love even his vices. And so I came. It was torture to be with him, but I was happy. . . . Only when he ordered me to compose an ode to our "happy reunion" did I lose control of myself. My humble apologies, Lo. Well, I was the only person alive to whom he could freely boast of his evil deeds. And he was responsible for many; he said he was the greatest man that ever lived, and therefore entitled to experience every sensation a man's body and mind are capable of. Yes, he seduced General Mo's concubine, and when the general had discovered it, Shao denounced him. Shao had been thinking of joining the conspiracy, but realized in time it was doomed to failure. He knew all the general's accomplices, but they didn't know him! The Censor praised Shao for his good advice—Shao told me that with relish! The general kept silent about him during the trial, because he had no written proof of Shao's interest in the conspiracy, and because he was too proud to bring up the adultery—and, anyway, the concubine had hanged herself, so that the general didn't have any proof in this case either. Shao loved to tell me about that old affair. . . . This spring he came to see me in the White Heron Monastery, for he liked nothing better than to gloat over the people he had reduced to misery. That's why he always made a point of visiting his illegitimate daughter in the fox shrine here, every time he passed through Chin-hwa. Told her she was leading a splendid life, with her loyal lover and her foxes.

'Well, what I said just now about my whipping that maid to death was perfectly true. Only read Shao for Soong. I never met that unfortunate student, only heard about him from Shao yesterday. Poor Saffron had told Shao everything about Soong, you see. Shao went to Soong's lodging late at night, knocked on his back door and told him he had information on General Mo's case. The student let him inside, and Shao killed him with an old carpenter's compass saw he had found among the rubbish by Soong's garden gate. He told me he had a dagger with him, but that it was always better to use a weapon found on the spot. That's why he killed the dancer with the scissors. Shao's only worry was that Soong might have got hold of evidence regarding Shao's adultery with his mother, perhaps old letters or something. He searched Soong's lodging, but there was nothing. Pour me another cup, Sexton!'

After she had emptied the wine cup, slowly this time, she went on:

'Needless to say, after Shao had helped me to bury the maid's body, I didn't tell him to go away! No, I begged him, begged him on my knees, to stay, to come back to me! He

168

replied he was sorry he hadn't seen me whipping her, but that it was his duty to report me to the authorities. He went away, laughing. I knew he would denounce me, and therefore I laid that clumsy false trail. When I was told about the anonymous letter, I knew that Shao had written it, and that he wanted to destroy me. He knew my stupid, abject devotion, knew I would never tell on him, even if my life depended on it!' Shaking her head despondently, she raised her hand and pointed at the pillar. 'See how I loved him! That poem there I composed when we were still together.'

Suddenly she glared at Judge Dee and snapped:

'When you were drawing your treacherous noose about him tighter and tighter, it was as if you were strangling me! Therefore I spoke up. Piecing together what I knew, I tried to save him. But you heard the last words he said.'

She set her wine cup down and rose. Putting her coiffure in order with a few deft movements of her shapely hands, she resumed casually:

'Now that Shao is dead, I could of course have said that it was he who whipped the maid to death. He was quite capable of doing just that. But now that he's dead, I want to die too. I could've thrown myself into the gorge after him, but that would have cost the sergeant there his life. Besides, somehow or other I have my pride too, and although I've done many things I shouldn't have done, I have never been a coward. I killed the maid, and I am going to take what's coming to me.' Turning to the Court Poet, she said with a faint smile, 'It has been a privilege to have known you, Chang, for you are a great poet. You, Sexton, I admire, because I've come to know you as a truly wise man. And I am grateful to you, Lo, for your staunch friendship. As to you, Magistrate Dee, I am sorry I snapped at you just now. My relationship with Shao was doomed to come to a disastrous end sooner or later, and you only did your duty. It's all for the best, for now that Shao had retired and could move about more freely than before, he was planning new evil deeds to keep himself amused. And I am finished anyway. Good-bye.'

She turned to the sergeant. He put the chains on her and led her away, followed by the two soldiers.

The Court Poet sat hunched up in his chair, his thin face a sickly grey. Slowly rubbing his forehead, he muttered:

'I've a splitting headache! And to think that I had been longing for a really shattering experience!' He got up and said brusquely, 'Let's go back to town, Lo.' Suddenly he smiled bleakly. 'Heavens, Lo, your career is made! The highest honours are in store for you, you'll be . . .'

'I know what's in store for me right now, sir,' the small magistrate interrupted dryly. 'Namely to sit at my desk for the rest of the night, writing my official report. Please go ahead to the palankeen, sir, I'll be with you in a moment.'

After the poet had gone, Lo gave the judge a long look. His lips twitching, he stammered:

'That . . . that was terrible, Dee. She . . . she . . .' His voice broke.

Judge Dee laid his hand lightly on his colleague's arm.

'You shall finish her biography, Lo, quoting every word she said just now. Thus your edition of her works will do full justice to her, and she shall live on in her poetry for generations to come. You go down together with Chang, for I'd like to stay here for a while, Lo. I need a little time to sort things out in my mind. Get the clerks to prepare everything in the chancery. Presently I shall join you there, give you a hand with drawing up all the official documents.' He looked after the departing magistrate for a while, then turned to the sexton and asked, 'What about you, sir?'

'I'll keep you company, Dee. Let's draw up our chairs to the balustrade, and enjoy the moon. We've come here to celebrate the Moon Festival, after all!'

The two men sat down, their backs to the half-cleared table. They were all alone in the pavilion, for as soon as Magistrate

Lo had left, the servants had slipped away to the kitchen in the forest, eager to discuss the strange happenings.

The judge silently stared at the mountain range opposite. He thought that in the eerie moonlight he could nearly distinguish every single tree. Suddenly he said:

'You are interested in Saffron, sir, the guardian of the Shrine of the Black Fox. I regret to inform you that she got rabies and died this afternoon.'

Sexton Loo nodded his large round head.

'I know. When I came up the mountain path I saw a black fox, for the first time in my life. Had one glimpse of its lithe, long shape, its sleek black fur. Then it streaked into the bushes and disappeared. . . .' He rubbed his stubbly cheeks, making a rasping sound. Still looking at the moon, he asked casually: 'Did you have definite proof against the Academician, Dee?'

'Not a shred, sir. But the poetess thought I had, and it was she who solved everything. If she hadn't spoken up, I would have blustered on for a while, my argument would have petered out with a vague theory. The Academician would have called it an interesting exercise in deduction, and that would've been the end of it. He knew perfectly well, of course, that I didn't have any proof against him. He killed himself not because he feared legal action, but only because his gigantic, superhuman pride would not allow him to live with the knowledge that someone pitied him.'

The sexton nodded again.

'It was quite a drama, Dee. A human drama, where foxes happened to act a part. But we shouldn't look at everything from the limited point of view of our small world of man. There are many other worlds, overlapping ours, Dee. From the point of view of the world of foxes, this was a fox drama, where a few human beings happened to act a minor part.'

'You may be right, sir. It seems to have begun about forty years ago, when Saffron's mother, then a young girl, brought a small black fox home. I don't know.' The judge stretched his long legs. 'I do know, however, that I am dog-tired!'

The other gave him a sidelong look.

'Yes, you'd better rest for a while, Dee. You and I, each in his own chosen direction, have still a long way to go. A very long and weary way.'

The sexton leaned back in his chair and looked up at the bright moon with his bulging, unblinking eyes.

POSTSCRIPT

JUDGE DEE was a historical person; he lived from 630 to 700 A.D., and was a brilliant detective and famous statesman of the Tang dynasty. The adventures related in the present novel are entirely fictitious, however, and the other characters introduced imaginary, with the exception of the poetess 'Yoo-lan'. For her I took as model the famous poetess Yü Hsüan-chi, who lived from ca. 844 to ca. 871. She was indeed a courtesan, who after a checkered career ended her life on the scaffold, accused of having beaten a maidservant to death; but the question of whether she was guilty or not has never been resolved. For more details about her career and her work, the reader is referred to my book *Sexual Life in Ancient China* (E. J. Brill, Leyden, 1961), pp. 172-175. The poem quoted on p. 155 of the present novel was actually written by her.

As regards some aspects of Chinese literary life mentioned in this story, it may be worth reminding the reader that for nearly two thousand years in China competitive literary examinations constituted the principal gate to a government career. Every citizen could take part in these examinations, and although, naturally, the sons of the well-to-do had better opportunities to prepare themselves for these tests than the sons of poor families, the fact that everyone who passed, regardless of social status and private means, was given an official appointment at once, lent the government system a democratic touch, and had a levelling influence on Chinese society. Literary achievements played a predominant role in social life, and among those calligraphy ranked very high; higher, as a matter of fact, than painting. This will be readily understood if one remembers that Chinese characters are largely ideographs which are painted rather than written;

one can legitimately compare calligraphy with Western abstract painting.

The three creeds of China were Confucianism, Taoism and Buddhism, the latter having been introduced into China from India in the first century A.D. Most officials were Confucianists with a sympathetic interest in Taoism, but largely anti-Buddhist. In the seventh century, however, a new Buddhist sect was introduced from India, which in China was called the Ch'an sect, and it absorbed many Taoist elements; it denied the Buddha as a saviour and declared all holy books useless, teaching that enlightenment must be found within one's own self. This doctrine was favoured by Chinese eclectic literati, and became popular also in Japan where it is known as Zen. Sexton Loo of the present novel was a Zen monk.

Chinese fox-lore dates from before the beginning of our era, and throughout the ages figured largely in Chinese literature. For more information on fox-magic I refer to *The Religious System of China*, the monumental work by the Dutch sinologue Prof. J. J. M. de Groot, Volume V, Book 2, pp. 576-600 (E. J. Brill, Leyden, 1910).

In Judge Dee's time the Chinese did not wear pigtails. That custom was imposed upon them after 1644 A.D. when the Manchus had conquered China. The men did their hair up in a top-knot, and they wore caps both inside and outside the house, taking their head gear off only when going to bed. To confront another person with one's head uncovered was a grave insult, the only exception being Taoist recluses and Buddhist priests. In the present novel this point is brought out in the murder of the student Soong.

In the Tang dynasty the Chinese did not smoke. Tobacco and opium were introduced into China many centuries after Judge Dee's time.

ROBERT VAN GULIK

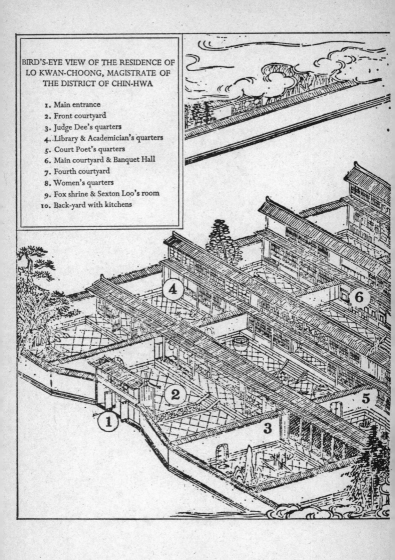

BIRD'S-EYE VIEW OF THE RESIDENCE OF
LO KWAN-CHOONG, MAGISTRATE OF
THE DISTRICT OF CHIN-HWA

1. Main entrance
2. Front courtyard
3. Judge Dee's quarters
4. Library & Academician's quarters
5. Court Poet's quarters
6. Main courtyard & Banquet Hall
7. Fourth courtyard
8. Women's quarters
9. Fox shrine & Sexton Loo's room
10. Back-yard with kitchens

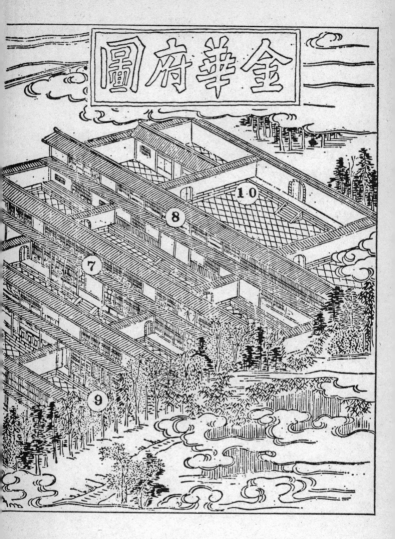

金華府圖